SHE WAS STUNNED BY HOW QUICKLY HE HAD AROUSED HER PASSION. . . .

Before she could speak, he leaned down and closed his mouth over hers, and then all she knew was the sweet sensation of him kissing her and feeling as if she were drowning in his kiss. Her eyes closed, and she reached out to put her arms around his neck, molding her body to his as she had done on the dance floor. Only now there was no pretense of dancing as they embraced. She wanted him, wanted him more than she could ever remember wanting any man. She wanted everything he had to give—no matter what the price. . . .

A CANDLELIGHT ECSTASY ROMANCE ®

INTERLUDE OF LOVE

Beverly Sommers

A CANDLELIGHT ECSTASY ROMANCE®

Published by
Dell Publishing Co., Inc.
1 Dag Hammarskjold Plaza
New York, New York 10017

Dell ® TM 681510, Dell Publishing Co., Inc.

Candlelight Ecstasy Romance®, 1,203,540, is a registered
trademark of Dell Publishing Co., Inc.,
New York, New York.

ISBN: 0-440-14521-X

Printed in the United States of America

First printing—August 1983

To Our Readers:

We have been delighted with your enthusiastic response to Candlelight Ecstasy Romances®, and we thank you for the interest you have shown in this exciting series.

In the upcoming months we will continue to present the distinctive sensuous love stories you have come to expect only from Ecstasy. We look forward to bringing you many more books from your favorite authors and also the very finest work from new authors of contemporary romantic fiction.

As always, we are striving to present the unique, absorbing love stories that you enjoy most—books that are more than ordinary romance.

Your suggestions and comments are always welcome. Please write to us at the address below.

Sincerely,

The Editors
Candlelight Romances
1 Dag Hammarskjold Plaza
New York, New York 10017

CHAPTER ONE

The telegram arrived while Jess was taking her morning hike. It was nearing November, and the Wyoming air had a bite to it that reddened her cheeks and made her think the first snow wouldn't be long in coming. With nothing more on her mind than setting in a supply of logs for the winter, she returned to her cabin and saw the insidious yellow envelope slipped halfway under her door.

And wouldn't Western Union be having a fit, she thought wryly, knowing their decided preference for calling in their messages to people with telephones instead of having to send their truck to hell and back up in the mountains. Utility companies and others of their ilk weren't happy about self-styled hermits who did without the modern amenities.

Well, Jess wasn't thrilled either. A telegram was one thing she could definitely live without, particularly a summons from Tanner Books, which this was sure to be. She pushed open the unlocked door, stooped to pick up the envelope, then put it in her back pocket for a bit so she could cool off. There would be plenty of time to read it after she had a cup of coffee, coffee she had judiciously made earlier and now only required a flame under the pot to warm it up.

While waiting for the coffee, she rolled up her bedroll from where she slept on the floor and stacked it in the corner, then opened the one window to let out some of the heat from the wood stove. She poured herself a mug of strong black coffee and took it over to the worktable that ran the length of the room. She had built it herself, along with some shelves above it for books. Jess sat down in her one chair—straight-backed and wooden—that she used for eating, typing, and reading, and drank half her coffee before reaching into her back pocket and bringing out the telegram.

It was addressed to Mr. Jess Haggerty, and that *Mr.* was the problem. A problem that seemed to be assuming larger proportions by the minute.

She tore open the envelope and reached inside for the message.

IMPERATIVE THAT YOU CONFIRM
IMMEDIATELY.
PROMOTION IN THE WORKS. AIRLINE AND
HOTEL
RESERVATIONS MADE. EXPECT YOU ON THE
FIRST.

It was signed Torrance Tyler III, her publisher, or TT3, which is how she always thought of him. She folded the telegram into an airplane, the way she used to do in the fifth grade, then threw it in the direction of the open window. It soared through, and she watched as it was caught by the wind and sailed out of sight. Unfortunately her problem didn't vanish with it.

"If I were Boots Ryan now," she said out loud, "I'd have a shot of whiskey to settle my nerves." She considered it for a moment, then decided that since she hadn't even had breakfast yet, she'd settle for a second cup of coffee. It didn't bother her at all that occasionally she spoke out loud; she decided she'd start to worry about it when she began answering herself.

Jess hadn't thought that wild horses would ever have been able to drag her away from her cabin in the mountains, but now it seemed that TT3 had the kind of horsepower that was not only going to drag her away from her cabin, but all the way to New York City, a place she had been more than willing to avoid in her lifetime. As far as she was concerned, Rocky Springs had too many people and too much civilization.

Anyway it had been a good couple of years while it lasted, and she had her cabin and sixteen acres all bought and paid for from the proceeds of her books. Still, she was sorry it had to come to an end, especially since she had a book in the works and another one infiltrating her thought processes. Generally she'd be starting work about now, but the telegram had thrown her off her schedule. And since her concentration was shot anyway, Jess thought she might as well drive down the mountain into town and send off a telegram to TT3—no matter *what* the consequences.

It had all started when she was graduated from college, applied for a job with the Department of Parks, and been hired as a fire watcher in the Rockies. She had been thrilled about the job when she had packed her bag and driven to the station that was to be her home. She would be living in her beloved Rocky Mountains, could use her free time to hunt and fish and explore the trails, and was sure her fellow workers would turn out to be kindred souls.

As for the last part, she soon found out that nothing could be further from the truth. Her fellow workers—all male—were born-and-bred westerners with decidedly old-fashioned views of women, and they resented having a woman thrust suddenly into their midst. At first, Jess recalled, there had been a lot of joking around, but she quickly saw that they thought she had been sent there expressly for their pleasure. She disabused them of that notion in a hurry, and it wasn't long before they left her strictly to herself. They didn't try to hinder her in her job, but they did as little as they could to help her.

So while the men sat around playing poker, which she was no longer invited to sit in on, or swapping stories about the women they had picked up in town on their days off, Jess would sit quietly in a corner and read. The available reading material in the station was magazines—the type with centerfolds—which didn't interest her at all, and a lot of dog-eared paperbacks, all of which were westerns.

The more Jess read, the more the westerns got her

10

blood boiling. Whoever had written them obviously didn't know the first thing about the West and had probably never seen a horse in person. At first she read them quickly, hoping they would improve in content. Then she began to read them more slowly, underlining all the discrepancies and formulating just what improvements were needed. Finally, in disgust, she gave up reading them altogether and began to think about writing one herself.

On her days off she began going into town and taking books about the Old West out of the library, consuming them slowly, taking copious notes of what she was learning, and then returning them for more the next week.

She developed a character in her mind—Boots Ryan—a solitary man with a quick draw and an eye for injustice, and she gave him all the attributes she thought a man should have. He was as unlike the men she worked with as she could possibly make him.

Since she had only had the minimum of required English courses in college and was doubtful of her writing ability, she visited the local college on one of her days off and signed up for a writing course that met one evening per week.

On the first night of her class Robert, the instructor, told them that everyone could write, and everyone had a story to tell. She felt an instant rapport with him. She also liked his dark, brooding good looks. All the students were told to bring in something they had written every week to be read and commented upon.

11

Slowly, patiently, Jess began to write her first western, written by hand late into the night. The men she worked with totally ignored what she was doing. They didn't ask what she was writing or even why she was writing. Sometimes she got the feeling she was invisible to them.

Every week Jess brought a new chapter to class, and after the third week she and Robert started going out after class for coffee and talked about writing. He was a poet who had been published in several literary magazines and was hoping to get a book of his poems published soon. He told Jess she had a natural writing style and encouraged her to keep it up.

By the sixth week Jess was in love with Robert, spending her nights off at his place in town and envisioning a future where the two of them would live in some secluded spot and write for a living.

Before the course had ended, she had finished the book and, after reading it over several times, was satisfied it was not only more authentic, but better written than the ones she had read. She had started writing it mainly to amuse herself in the lonely hours when she was off duty but still required to remain at the station. But now, with Robert's encouragement, she took it to town and paid to have it typed, then sent it off to New York to the publisher who had put out several of the books she had so thoroughly criticized.

To her amazement a contract from the publisher arrived a couple of months later along with a letter from the publisher himself, Torrance Tyler III, asking her if she'd be interested in doing a series based around her central character, Boots Ryan. The letter was addressed to Mr. Jess Haggerty—which didn't escape Jess's notice. All the westerns she had read had been written by men, and she thought it prudent to let Mr. Tyler go on thinking she was male. Jess signed the contract, answered the letter in the affirmative, and that was the start of her writing career. It was, however, the end of her romance.

Robert, who had previously done nothing but encourage her, now referred to her writing as "pulp," even "trash," and got very defensive about the fact that Jess had earned more money with one book than he made from both teaching and the sale of his poems. Robert was the second man she had been in love with; he was also the second man to shoot her down after having previously done nothing but encourage her.

Mark, whom she had dated all through college, who had spent all his time with her hunting and fishing and climbing the mountains, and who had always known about and encouraged her ambition to work for the Park Department, had looked at her in amazement when she refused to move with him to Houston, where he wanted to take an advanced degree.

"If you loved me, you'd go with me," he had said to her.

"I could say the same to you, Mark," she had said, but of course he hadn't thought it was the same thing at all. After all, he was the man, wasn't he?

To have it happen to her twice was too much. At that point Jess swore off men. With the money from the advance, she bought herself a secondhand typewriter and a typing manual, taught herself to type, and sold three more books to Tanner within the year. Then, with money in the bank and a great desire to see the last of her co-workers, she bought herself an abandoned cabin in the mountains along with sixteen acres of woodland and her own stream, and moved in. From then on she lived the life of a virtual hermit, which didn't bother her a bit. Not if being a hermit meant she didn't have to associate with the kind of obnoxious men she had been thrown into contact with at the station, or the kind who always thought the man's work came first or that the man had to be more successful.

She had lost contact with friends she had made in college, most of whom were married now, and she had no social life. Her parents, both college professors, had taken early retirements and moved to Hawaii, and while she corresponded with them frequently, she hadn't seen them in over a year. She found she savored her solitary existence and derived a great deal of pleasure from her writing. The mountains were also an endless source of pleasure to her; she never tired of climbing them and exploring the different trails. She was happy and content with her life and, with an innate optimism, had somehow thought it would go on forever.

Then two weeks ago the letter from Torrance Tyler III had arrived. It had extended an invitation to her to come to New York for a Christmas promotion of her latest book. It would mean personal appearances in bookstores, a couple of radio interviews, and a slot on a television talk show. He had added in a handwritten note on the bottom of the letter that he was looking forward to showing his favorite author the big city.

Jess had ignored the letter, hoping the publishers would change their minds. And it wasn't as though they could call and plead with her, because she didn't have a telephone. The infrequent correspondence she received from Tanner Books—which consisted mostly of contracts and checks—was all sent to her post office box in town.

A second letter had arrived a week ago, stating that the trip was, of course, paid for by the publishers. Another handwritten note had appeared stating that Mr. Tyler had located an authentic western bar in the city, where Jess was sure to feel at home.

He probably expects me to shoot it up, she had thought to herself in amusement, stifling the impulse to write back and tell him she didn't feel at home in any bar. Instead, she had thrown the letter in the wood stove and watched it burn, wondering if her writing career was also going up in smoke.

Now the telegram had come. Jess wasn't one to hide her head under the pillow, so she reasoned she'd just have to go to New York and brazen it out with the publishers. After all, she had never actually *said* she was a man. It hadn't stated anywhere in her contracts that she *had* to be a man. Jess *was* her name, or at least the name she had always gone by. And if things turned out the way she figured they'd turn out, she might be able to turn around and fly back to Wyoming the same day. If there was one thing she *wasn't* interested in seeing, it was that large, notorious city filled with crime and smog and God knows what else, even if it did have an authentic western bar. From what she had seen of New York in movies, though, the bar was probably filled with "midnight cowboys."

She also figured she owed Tanner Books a debt of gratitude for enabling her to quit her job, buy her cabin, and retire to her peaceful life. If, after meeting her, they were no longer interested in buying her books, well, she could always write other kinds. Maybe romances. Those authors all appeared to be women. On the other hand she probably couldn't. She now knew a lot about the Old West, but she knew virtually nothing about romance, at least the happily-ever-after kind.

It was with great reluctance that she finally got up and headed down the mountain in her Jeep to send a telegram in reply.

Kennedy Airport was total confusion, and Jess, not having been met at the gate as she had anticipated, made her way downstairs to retrieve the large backpack she hadn't been allowed to carry on the plane. The people surging toward the luggage conveyor reminded her of a cattle stampede, and unwilling to push or shove her way through, she stood off at a distance and waited for the crowd to diminish. She was still waiting when she heard her name being announced over the public address system, and a porter pointed out a telephone for her to pick up.

16

"This is Jess Haggerty." She spoke into the phone, hoping it was someone to meet her.

There was silence for a long moment. Then came a hesitant female voice. "Are you sure?"

She had been right and they were expecting a man. "Of course, I'm sure," she responded, glad it wasn't TT3 at the other end. "Who is this?"

Another pause. "Are you Jess Haggerty the writer? For Tanner Books?"

Jess flushed with pleasure at hearing herself called "the writer." No one ever referred to her like that at home. If she was referred to at all it was probably as "that hermit up in the mountains." "Yes, I am," she said into the phone.

"Oh, my gosh! We were expecting a man!" Then the voice turned into laughter, and Jess found herself joining in.

"Well, I'm sorry to disappoint you, but I'm not a man," she said firmly. Maybe now she would be able to turn right around and go home. She felt bad enough out of her element in the airport; the city was bound to be worse.

The girl had got her laughter under control. "I'm Allison, Mr. Tyler's assistant, and I'm supposed to be meeting you. I kept watching for a cowboy to get off the plane and completely missed you. Where are you now?"

It didn't sound as though she were going to be sent back just yet. "I'm waiting for my luggage."

"Okay. Stay there and I'll be right down. Oh, listen, how will I recognize you?"

Jess looked around. "You won't have any trouble,

I'm practically the only one left. But just in case, I'm about five five, I've got copper-colored hair, and I'm wearing a sheepskin jacket."

The phone disconnected in her ear, and Jess went over to the conveyor and waited for the oversize lone backpack that was going around in circles. She lifted it off, slipped her arms through the straps, then turned around to see a young woman hurrying toward her.

Jess could hardly take her eyes off the bizarre pair of cowboy boots the woman was wearing. They were of gold leather with red fringe that came to the hemline of a blue denim skirt with a ruffle around the bottom. Cowboys must be in style this year, she thought, if such a fancy outfit could really be termed "cowboy." She lifted her glance to a small elfin face with short, ragged brown hair and enormous brown eyes. The woman was tiny, making Jess feel like a rangy horse in comparison.

"I'm Allison," said the elf, "and are you ever a surprise. You're going to hit the office like a bombshell, and I can't wait to see the fireworks." Her eyes seemed to be positively dancing at the thought.

Jess could wait. Feeling very uncomfortable about her duplicity, she thought seriously of turning around right then and taking the next plane out, but already Allison was hurrying her outside the terminal and into a taxi, giving the driver an address in the East Thirties.

When they were on their way, Allison looked over at Jess and winked. "Welcome to New York and sorry about the foul-up at the airport."

Jess grinned at her. "Thanks, but what's going to happen now? Will I be instantly deported back to Wyoming for not being a man?"

Allison looked impish. "Well, maybe not. . . . Mr. Tyler does have an affinity for women." Then, seeing Jess's expression, she burst out laughing. "I was only kidding. Not about his liking women, but this is different. This is *business.* You are certainly going to raise his blood pressure by several degrees though."

"I really don't see what all the fuss is about," said Jess, trying her best to assume an innocent look. "Women are certainly as capable of writing westerns as men, aren't they?"

Allison could hardly contain her mirth. "The difference is that you were Mr. Tyler's discovery, and he's got you pictured as some lean, leathery cowboy type—something of a recluse, I believe, living all alone out in Wyoming with only your horse for company. And what's worse, he's had an entire ad campaign built around that image."

Since that almost perfectly fitted Jess's own image of herself—except for the gender and the fact she had a Jeep instead of a horse—she began to think that TT3 was rather astute. She wondered briefly whether he fitted her picture of the cultured gentleman of publishing with, perhaps, a bit of silver at his temples, a tweedy jacket with leather elbow patches, and horn-rimmed glasses.

"How extensive is the ad campaign?" asked Jess.

"Oh, press releases, ads in the papers, radio spots —that kind of thing. Luckily none of it has gone out yet, but it was ready to go as soon as you arrived."

19

Jess slid down in her seat, a feeling of guilt sweeping over her. All that work, all that expense, and all because she had let them believe she was a man. A fleeting thought of disguising herself as a man swept across her mind, but was instantly rejected as being too cowardly. She was just going to have to take the consequences of her deception.

Jess glanced out the rear window of the taxi. The ride through Queens was rather monotonous but then she could see Manhattan across the river and the sight of the famous skyline was fairly breathtaking. Not as beautiful as the Rockies, of course, but awesome just the same. "That's really something, isn't it?" she breathed.

Allison looked surprised. "You've never been to New York before?"

"I've never been out of Wyoming before," Jess admitted. "Except for a couple of skiing trips to Colorado." And if she had any say in the matter, she was never going to leave Wyoming again.

"Just relax and enjoy yourself," Allison told her. "This isn't your fault, and even if Mr. Tyler goes off the wall when he sees you, you're one of our most popular authors, and no one's going to stay mad at you for long."

Except Jess knew it was partly her fault. They might have assumed in error that she was a man, but she had aided and abetted them in that assumption. Her irrepressible humor surfaced. "Perhaps I could dress up like a cowboy. I could put my hair up under a hat and talk in a deep voice. Maybe even wear a false mustache." Cowardly, true, she thought—but why not?

Allison looked at Jess's thickly lashed eyes, lovely smooth skin and delicately curved mouth, all bereft of makeup, and laughed out loud. "No way! Anyway it's our problem, not yours."

They exited from the Midtown Tunnel into Manhattan and Jess spent the rest of the ride viewing the crowds and stores and sights of the city that seemed familiar to her as a result of so many movies and television programs she had seen as a child that had been set there. It was truly fantastic, she mused, but she wouldn't want to live there. She'd probably become claustrophobic just visiting for a few days.

Tanner Books occupied an entire brownstone on East 38th Street. Jess had expected a modern glass-and-steel office building and was surprised when the cab dropped them off in front of what looked to be an old house. Allison led her up carpeted stairs to a reception area furnished with antiques, where a slim young blonde was seated behind a desk typing.

Allison took Jess over to the desk and waited for the girl to look up. When she did, Allison gave her a mischievous look. "Guess who this is, Linda."

Linda wasn't amused. "I don't know, but Mr. Tyler's going to have a heart attack if you don't show up with the cowboy soon. He's been buzzing me every two minutes to see if you're back yet."

Allison couldn't stifle a giggle. "*This* is the cowboy! Jess, meet Linda. She's Mr. Tyler's secretary."

Jess held out her hand, but the girl was clearly too

21

confused to respond. She just stared at Jess, shaking her head in disbelief.

Allison chortled. "Aren't you going to announce her, Linda? Better not keep the boss waiting."

Linda shook her head. "Not me, Alli. You're the one who showed up with her, *you* explain her. He's going to be so mad when he finds out, he'll fire anyone in the vicinity. You know how he goes on about that old cowboy."

Jess smiled at the description of herself.

Allison seemed to be losing some of her humor as she looked at Jess, her bottom lip between her teeth. "Would you like to freshen up first or anything?"

"You don't have time," Linda muttered.

Jess shook her head. "No, that's not necessary."

Allison glanced at her backpack. "Why don't you at least leave that out here?"

Jess shrugged out of her backpack and placed it in a corner of the reception area. She was beginning to feel like a child who had been bad and was being sent to the principal's office. And she'd been bad enough times to clearly remember the feeling.

Allison sighed. "Well, come on, I guess we better get it over with."

Jess's legs felt as if they had been climbing mountains for hours. With a sinking sensation in her stomach now that the moment had finally arrived, she followed Allison through a door, down a long carpeted hallway, and then inside an office, whereupon Allison did a disappearing act, leaving Jess standing alone to face the occupant of the office.

CHAPTER TWO

At first Jess didn't notice anything but the man behind the desk, and he was on the phone, half turned to the window behind him and didn't see her enter. He was the most irresistibly attractive man she had ever seen, and she walked toward his desk as though drawn by a magnet. What was so astounding about the man's looks was that he almost exactly fitted the description in Jess's books of Boots Ryan—a description that encompassed her ideal in a man. He had the same curly dark hair, cut slightly long; the thick dark brows; the hawkish nose; the hard, chiseled mouth. . . .

Her movement must have caught his eye as he immediately turned to face her, and she saw that his eyes were dark like Boots's too. It was as if her character had come to life. The only difference was that Boots wouldn't have been caught dead in a three-piece suit and tie.

The man abruptly terminated his phone call before leaning back in his leather chair and slowly surveying her, a look of enjoyment on his face.

Then his harsh features relaxed in a warm smile as

23

he caught her embarrassed look. "What can I do for you, dear?"

His voice wasn't anything like Boots's. It was fast and clipped, with traces of an eastern accent, not the soft, slow drawl of a man of the West. Jess flushed at his easy use of the endearment, reminded of the men at the station. And, like them, he seemed to be staring at her as though she were a cow at auction.

Jess took a deep breath and tried to calm herself. She mustn't let the fact that he so closely resembled Boots affect her; after all, Boots was a figment of her own imagination. And if his attitude reminded her of the station men, well, men were probably the same the world over when it came to women.

"I'm Jess Haggerty, Mr. Tyler," she told him matter-of-factly, then felt a sense of satisfaction as she watched his look change quickly from one of pure male interest to one of incredulity. *Score one for me,* Jess thought to herself.

His black eyes narrowed, and his face took on a dangerous look. "Tell me you're joking, honey. Who put you up to this? Allison? Linda?"

Jess ignored the *honey* for the moment. She could tell he knew it was the truth by the resignation in his voice. She stood there not saying anything. His signatures on letters had become so familiar to her that she had thought of him as an old friend and was sorry that their first meeting had turned out to be such a disappointment to him. But then she was disappointed too; she had expected an older gentleman who would treat her with the respect she thought an author deserved. But how astonishing that he should so closely resemble Boots!

He just stared at her for a few moments, seemingly at a loss as to what to do, and then he lifted the phone and pushed a button. "Tell Allison to get the hell in here," he growled into the mouthpiece before slamming it back down.

A more subdued Allison than Jess had previously seen entered the office and stood beside Jess. "You wanted to see me, Tory?"

Tory, Jess thought. Yes, that fits him.

"Explain the joke to me, Alli," he said to his assistant. To Jess his silky tones sounded dangerously ominous.

Allison shifted nervously on her feet, not looking Tory in the eye but past his head, fixing her gaze out the window. "It's not a joke, Tory," she mumbled.

Tory leaned back in his swivel chair and ran his fingers through his thick hair, his eyes never leaving Allison. "All right," he said, his manner decisive. "Cancel the reservation at the Algonquin. Get the publicity poster removed from the lobby. Cancel the cocktail party in the suite. And get her another reservation somewhere else—preferably under another name."

"Right, Tory," said Allison, moving quickly out of the office.

Jess stood calmly as Tory took an intricately carved pipe from a stand on his desk, slowly filled it with tobacco, then lighted it, watching her through the smoke. "Have a seat until I figure out what to do with you," he said at last, clearly displeased by her presence.

Jess looked around for a chair. She had never seen so many books before except in a library, and she wasn't sure the library at Rocky Springs had this many. They were piled up on his brown leather couch and on every available chair and were even spilling out of the bookshelves that covered two of the walls.

"Just move some of the books," he told her impatiently, and Jess moved a stack of them off one of the chairs and onto the floor before seating herself. It was warm in the office, and she undid her jacket and slipped it off, pushing it to fit over the back of the chair.

She ignored him, looking instead around the office, noting several of her book covers framed beneath glass on the paneled walls. The room, she noted with surprise, had something of a western decor. Remington prints hung over the fireplace and there was even a deerhead mounted in one corner of the room, the antlers used as a coat rack. She knew Tanner Books specialized in books of the West, but it was still surprising that his office resembled a cowboy's abode more than any of the houses she had been in in Wyoming. Most of the people out there went in for modern styles.

Tory was staring at her, his eyes unfathomable. She assumed that he was trying to intimidate her, which just wasn't going to work. She wasn't intimidated by bears or rattlesnakes or . . . well, by anything. Certainly not by a mere man. If men had intimidated her, she wouldn't have lasted at her job for a day, let alone the year she had been there.

She gave him what she hoped was a pleasant smile. At least one of them could observe the amenities. "It's a pleasure meeting you at last, Mr. Tyler," she said sweetly.

She observed a dangerous glint in his eyes, then he threw back his head and was suddenly laughing. Despite her annoyance with him she felt her mouth widening in response, and then she was laughing, too, for no reason at all except that he seemed absolutely charming when he laughed.

"Jess Haggerty," he mused, shaking his head in disbelief, the smile wide on his face. "I had you pictured as some mangy old cowboy, and here you show up, a pretty kid out of nowhere. Hell, I even had Jess Haggerty jokes I used to tell."

"I'm no kid," she informed him coolly, "and I'd love to hear the jokes." She crossed her jean-clad legs and wished she could pull off her Frye boots and get comfortable.

"They're not for mixed company," he murmured. "How old were you when you wrote your first book for us?"

"Twenty-three."

She watched while he did some mental arithmetic to come up with her present age of twenty-five.

His eyes narrowed as he drew thoughtfully on his pipe, filling the room to suffocation point as far as Jess was concerned. His pipe seemed to make more smoke than her wood stove. She longed to open the window behind him and let in some fresh air—assuming there was such a thing in New York.

"It occurs to me that when I wrote you last year requesting a picture of yourself for the book jacket, you politely refused."

Jess didn't answer; she remembered the letter well.

"At the time," he went on in a deceptively mild tone of voice, "I thought you were a shy old geezer protecting your anonymity."

Jess was trying to maintain the kind of straight face she had used to such good effect during poker games.

He suddenly leaned across his desk. "You conned me, didn't you?"

"I beg your pardon?" said Jess, her voice also deceptively calm. She certainly didn't consider herself a con artist, if that's what he was implying.

"What's your real name? Jessica?"

She nodded.

"And yet you signed your book Jess and let me believe you were a man."

"I've always been called Jess," she protested.

"And those notes of mine. You must have gotten a lot of laughs out of them."

She could barely contain the smile that was trying to form on her lips. "I can't wait to see the authentic western bar," she said, a wicked gleam in her green eyes.

"Touché," he murmured, an answering gleam in his own. He picked up the telephone. "Alli? Get together with Manny and come up with something.

We'll be at lunch." He hung up and looked at Jess. "Did they feed you on the plane?"

They had, but it had been a miniature meal, and Jess was starving. "I could eat," she said.

He got up from behind his desk and grabbed his coat off the antlers. Jess stood up and put on her jacket, noting that Tory was several inches taller than herself. And rather than having the long, rangy look of her cowboy hero, he was muscular. She wondered how a city man managed to stay so fit. She would have thought he'd be soft from sitting behind a desk all day. Maybe he played tennis or polo, she thought: one of those fancy eastern sports.

"Indian okay?" he asked her, propelling her out the door of the office.

"Indian?" What was the man talking about?

"There's an Indian restaurant down the street. Good food and not too fattening."

She looked down at herself, wondering if he was suggesting she needed to diet. And then dismissed the thought; she knew she didn't have an extra ounce of fat on her. She might eat well, but her hikes in the mountains burned it all off.

With visions of buffalo meat dancing around in her head, she followed him out of the building on the way to the Indian restaurant.

Once seated in the dim interior of the restaurant, Jess glanced around with interest. One table held a group of men wearing turbans. The hostess had worn a sari, lovely and altogether exotic to Jess.

"I thought you meant *Indian*," she said, taking the menu that was being handed to her.

"This *is* Indian."

"I thought you meant *American* Indian."

Tory choked on the water he was drinking. "I didn't know they had restaurants."

"They don't as far as I know. But I never thought about the other kind."

He looked amused. "No *India* Indians in Wyoming?"

"Not that I've ever seen. I guess they don't go in for ranching."

"It would be impractical—seeing as how they consider cows sacred."

She was studying the menu. It appeared to be written in English and yet she didn't understand a word of it. "I don't recognize one thing. Would you mind ordering for me?"

He smiled in understanding. "I felt the same way the first time. What would you like to drink? How about a Manhattan?"

She shook her head. "Whiskey's fine."

"Whiskey and soda?"

"Just on the rocks."

He chuckled. "Now you sound like the Jess Haggerty I expected. 'He liked his whiskey neat and his women with all the trimmings,' " he said, quoting from one of her books. He called over one of the waiters and ordered their drinks.

"Where I come from," said Jess with an innocent look, "Manhattans are considered an old lady's drink."

"If you're trying to raise my ire, you're not going to succeed." His gaze on her was steady.

The waiter brought their drinks, and Jess quickly downed her whiskey, feeling the warmth remove her tenseness. She began to relax, thinking the worst was over. She had appeared, they had found out she was a woman, and the world hadn't come to a standstill. It was beginning to look as though things were going to work out. Certainly TT3 couldn't be very upset if he was taking her out to lunch.

Tory gave the waiter their order, then viewed her over the top of his drink. "So tell me, what do you do out in Wyoming besides write?"

Jess shrugged. "I read."

He looked disbelieving. "That's all you do? Just read and write?"

She nodded. "Mostly. I also hike a lot, and mountain climb, and hunt and fish."

He was suddenly looking at her as though she were an alien from outer space. "Good Lord, all of that? Is that your idea of fun?"

She smiled at his incredulous tone. "The hiking and climbing are—I hunt and fish for my food."

He was shaking his head in disbelief. "Don't they have stores in Rocky Springs?"

She laughed. "A couple. But I don't live in Rocky Springs."

"That's where we send your mail."

"Oh, I have a post-office box there, but I live up in the mountains. And I do buy some of my food, but my goal is to become self-sufficient."

He was looking truly amazed. "What are you, some kind of recluse?"

31

"I suppose so, but it suits me; I don't need other people."

"At the risk of offending you, I have to say I think that's a real waste."

Jess frowned. "A waste of what?"

Tory's eyes were warm. "Let's just say I'm glad *all* the beautiful women in the world aren't hidden away up in the mountains trying to be self-sufficient."

Jess ignored the compliment. He probably thought a woman needed a man to get along in life. Well, she knew differently. "Maybe they'd be happier if they were," she said to him.

Their eyes locked for a moment, and then something stirred in his depths. "I have a feeling you don't know very much about life yet, honey," he said softly.

"On the contrary, Mr. Tyler. I know more about it than I wish to know," she said, "and if you persist in calling me *honey* and *dear,* I refuse to be responsible for my actions." If more women were independent like herself, Jess thought, they wouldn't have to contend with the way men treated them. She wouldn't trade the way she lived to be the wife of any one of them. Not that she had seemed to be what any of them had been looking for in a wife. She gathered the men where she came from liked their women sweet and submissive. Probably not much different from New Yorkers in that respect.

"I apologize, it's just my way of speaking," Tory was saying. "Anyway I think we know each other well enough to use first names, don't you?"

"I'd find it a big improvement over *honey*," said Jess, then felt the involuntary smile form on her lips.

"What's so funny, Jess?"

"It's just that all this time I've been thinking of you as TT Three," she said with a rueful grin.

He reached over and placed his hand on top of hers, making her feel like she'd been touched by an electric wire. "Start thinking of me as Tory, all right?"

She nodded, pulling her hand from beneath his. Well, maybe it *was* electricity; it was a dry day, and that often caused— *Oh, quit trying to con yourself, Jess,* she said to herself. *There's a physical attraction here, maybe because of his resemblance to Boots, maybe not, but there's no use denying it. But it doesn't mean you have to do anything about it. Just keep in mind the man's your publisher, and this is a* business *lunch.*

With a look that showed he sensed her discomfort Tory changed the subject. "Tell me, how did you become so literate, living out there in the middle of nowhere?"

What did he think, that she was born a hermit? Jess thought of her parents and her college education. "What do you want, Tory, my life story?"

He laughed out loud. "If I recall correctly, I tried to get that from you along with a picture. You ignored my request."

"I didn't think it would make interesting reading," she said, recalling that letter very well. At the time she had briefly thought of making up a life story

33

suitable for the author of westerns, but had decided she wasn't capable of *that* much deceit.

"I beg to differ. I have a feeling you're probably endlessly fascinating."

Beautiful? And now fascinating? She was finding it hard to believe a sophisticated New Yorker like Tory could think either one fitted her. There he was, looking like one of those men you saw in magazine advertisements, and she was wearing an old flannel shirt because she hadn't felt like spending the money for a new one.

"I don't think the details of one's life are what is important, Mr. Tyler. It's the way one thinks about things, and you should be able to discern that from my writing. I think I've put most of my beliefs and philosophy in my books."

He was nodding. "Umm. But at the time I read your manuscripts, I was picturing the author as being a man. . . . I think I'll have to go back and reread them with you in mind. As I recall, Boots is a loner, doesn't believe in getting close to people. . . ."

The conversation came to a halt as the food began to arrive at their table. And just in time, thought Jess. She really didn't feel like getting into a conversation regarding her aversion to relationships.

Tory seemed to know half the people in the restaurant, and as they were eating, she watched him greet people who stopped by the table to say hello. He would gesture to her, saying, "One of my writers," but he didn't introduce her to anyone. She liked the fast way he talked, his New York accent, and the way he gestured with his hands when he spoke. He was completely different from any man she had known before, and she found the difference intriguing. The food was also completely different from anything she had ever eaten, but the spicy dishes were delicious, and she finished them all.

When they had finished, he ordered coffee. "How about some dessert?" he asked.

"I'd love some," said Jess, having noticed some delicious-looking concoctions being eaten by the people at the next table and dying to try some.

He lifted a quizzical brow. "You're not on a diet?"

No one had ever suggested to her that she needed to go on a diet, and she flashed him a look of annoyance.

He lifted both hands and assumed an innocent air. "I didn't mean anything by that. It's just that all the women I know are always on diets."

She found herself wondering how many women he knew, then decided it was really none of her business.

He ordered dessert for both of them and watched appreciatively while she ate hers. "My mother would love you," he told her. "She never thinks anyone eats enough."

Jess wasn't sure whether that was a compliment or a slur on her eating habits, so she let it pass. She drank her black coffee, noting the large amounts of sugar and cream he dumped in his. One thing in New York's favor was the food, she decided. However, with no mountains in the vicinity to climb to work off the calories, she just might have to diet if she stayed in the city very long.

Tory leaned back in his chair with a satisfied sigh. "Enjoy the lunch?"

"Very much."

"Good. We'll come back here again."

Jess excused herself to go to the ladies' room, and as she washed her hands and smoothed down her hair that had been blown awry by the New York wind, she wondered at the attraction Tory held for her, for she was undeniably attracted to him. Mark had been her buddy—someone with whom she shared activities; Robert and she had writing in common and what she had thought of as an intellectual rapport. But with Tory . . . she hesitated to put a label on it. To be honest with herself, and she generally was, with Tory it was out-and-out physical.

She returned to find Tory engaged in conversation with a well-dressed woman of indeterminate age. Jess tried to tune out the conversation and shifted uncomfortably in her chair as she watched them talk. She could see that the woman was also attracted to Tory. Her dark eyes held a challenging look, and she kept touching him on the arm as she spoke. Jess looked over the woman's elegant clothes with appreciation but no envy. She supposed she could package herself that well, too, if she wanted to expend the necessary time, energy, and of course, expense. But she didn't. And it was probably all in the cause of attracting a man anyway. Jess wasn't interested in attracting a man.

The woman's gaze lighted on Jess for a moment, and Jess smiled, but then the woman was leaning down and offering her cheek for Tory to kiss before moving off toward the restaurant exit.

Jess felt a flash of something suspiciously like jealousy flare through her momentarily before she forced it to subside. Well, she didn't know what that woman's problem was, but she had a good idea about the reason for her own attraction for Mr. Tory Tyler the Third. It had been two years since she had been with a man, and she guessed her hormones were finally catching up with her. And then of course, there was that uncanny resemblance to Boots. . . .

She should have stayed in Wyoming, where she rarely even saw a man, unless you could count old Mort Babcock at the general store. Or Mr. Johnson at the post office. . . .

Jess shook herself out of her reverie and saw that Tory was eying her in an amused fashion and that somehow someone had poured her a second cup of coffee without her noticing.

Jess took a sip of the coffee and decided it was time for *her* to initiate some of the small talk.

"What about you? What do *you* do when you're not working?" she asked Tory.

"I read a lot. Some for work, some for pleasure."

"That's all? Just work and read?" she asked, lifting one brow in imitation of him.

"There's a lot to do in New York," he said in what she construed to be an evasive answer.

"Like what?" If he could be nosy about her life, she could do the same, Jess reasoned.

"Oh, there's concerts and the opera and theater.

And in publishing someone's always giving a party. And ballet and—"

"*Ballet?*" she said, interrupting him.

He smiled. "I know—in Wyoming that would be considered an old lady's activity, right?"

Worse than that, thought Jess, but didn't say it. It sounded like he kept busy. It also sounded like the kind of things one didn't do alone, but then she didn't figure a good-looking man like Tory probably *had* to do them alone.

Tory summoned the waiter for their check. "I'd love to spend all afternoon talking to you, but right now we'd better get back to the office and get the meeting with Manny over with." He gave the waiter a credit card, then stood up and helped her on with her jacket.

"Who's Manny?" she asked.

"My partner. He handles the business end, I handle the editorial. He's the one who set up the publicity campaign for you, only it wasn't you we had in mind."

He signed for the meal, then made an attempt to open the restaurant door for her, but she was already through it. She looked at the crowds fighting for space on the sidewalk and wondered at so many people wanting to live on one small piece of land. She would have liked to get some exercise, to walk off the effects of the lunch, but Tory was hustling her straight back to the office. Jess had her fingers crossed, hoping that Manny had come up with a solution.

CHAPTER THREE

Linda was sitting at her desk eating a sandwich and reading a fashion magazine.

"Where's Manny and Alli?" Tory asked her.

"In your office waiting for you."

Torry was about to go to his office when he noticed Jess's backpack where she had left it in a corner. "What's that? Get it out of here, Linda, it's not adding anything to the decor."

"Oh, I don't know," drawled Jess. "A backpack from the West in an office decorated in western decor." At Tory's look she added, "It's mine. My luggage."

Tory strode over and looked down at it. "This is your *luggage?*"

She nodded. "It's all I had. I never go anywhere except up in the mountains, and that's what I use. There were smaller ones on the plane just like it. Honest. Mine was apparently considered too big for carry-on luggage."

He gave her a wry smile. "I apologize. And believe me, you're one of a kind." He turned to his secretary.

39

"Can you believe that, Linda? A woman traveling with just a backpack?"

Linda didn't even acknowledge the remark, much to Jess's amusement.

Tory took Jess back to his office, where he introduced her to Manny, a bear of a man with a cherubic face that Jess found appealing. On Manny's part he didn't seem at all pleased by *her* appearance.

"*This* is your cowboy?" he practically screamed at Tory. "*This* is supposed to be your authentic cowboy right off the range? Tell me what we're going to do, Tory. Just tell me that, will you?"

Tory ignored the outburst, going behind his desk and slowly and calmly lighting his pipe. Allison was perched on a corner of Tory's desk, and Manny started pacing around the room, bypassing all the stacks of books. Jess removed her jacket and leaned back against the door, feeling as though she were observing a scene in a movie. She had never seen a more nervous man than Manny, who was now lighting a new cigarette, not even noticing he already had one in his other hand.

Tory got his pipe lighted and looked up. "I was hoping you'd come up with something while we were at lunch," he said to Manny.

Manny's face was turning red. "Come up with something? Just like that, Tory? Like what miracle did you think I would work while you were out enjoying yourself? Have *I* had lunch? Has *Alli* had lunch? I don't believe this is happening. I just don't believe it!"

Manny turned to Jess. "Why the hell aren't you a cowboy?"

"Because I'm a writer," said Jess, and he gave her a look of grudging admiration.

"And one of our best," added Tory.

"I have an idea," said Allison softly, but the two men ignored her.

Just like being back at the station, thought Jess. No one ever pays any attention to a woman when she has something to say.

"We're just going to have to scrap the campaign," Tory said decisively.

"Scrap the campaign?" yelled Manny. "That was the biggest thing we had going for the Christmas season. We've already bought time, made all the arrangements. Do you want to be the one to justify the cost to our stockholders? And don't look at me—this was *your* baby, *you* think of something."

"I think I have an idea," said Allison again, a little louder this time, but only Jess was listening.

"We could change the campaign," said Tory. "Maybe use Cody Montana."

A look of distaste crossed Jess's face, but no one was looking at her. Cody Montana was one of the writers she had criticized so thoroughly.

"*Cody Montana?*" Manny was turning even redder. "First of all he's an alcoholic, or had you forgotten? Second of all he lives in Italy. Thirdly, if I recall correctly, you were going to drop him because he's become a lousy writer. Look, Tory, we've got a western series and no cowboy. That's the story, and that's what we've got to work with."

41

Allison slid off the desk and faced Tory. "I've got an idea."

"Great, let's hear it," said Tory to Jess's surprise. Was he really going to listen to a woman's opinion?

"Couldn't we hire an actor?"

Tory spread out his hands. "What are you talking about, Alli?"

"An actor. You could hire an actor to play the part of Jess. You know, dress up like a cowboy, make all the public appearances—"

"Hey, I like that," said Manny in a normal tone of voice. "I think that just might have possibilities. Good thinking, Alli!"

Jess was beginning to see that this office didn't exactly work the way the station had after all. If she had ever put forth a suggestion there, the men would have laughed her out of the station. Or worse.

"It wouldn't work," said Tory softly.

"Yeah?" said Manny. "Well, find me something that *will* work. Listen, if you're worried about word of it leaking out, we can sign him to a contract. Sue him if he talks. Hell, any actor would be glad of the work, particularly so close to Christmas. Am I right, Alli?"

Allison nodded.

Tory leaned back in his chair. "You're forgetting, Manny, he's going to have to go on talk shows—talk about the books. And answer questions in the book-stores. What actor is going to know anything about the books, or how they were written, or enough about the Old West in general?"

"Yeah," said Manny, sounding depressed. "Yeah, Tory, you got a point."

"Jess could coach him," suggested Allison.

"Right," said Manny. "The cowgirl here could coach him. They could hole up in a hotel for a few days, he could read the books, she could tell him everything he needs to know. Hell, actors are supposed to be able to improvise anyway."

Allison looked over at Jess. "Of course, it's really up to Jess, and I wouldn't blame her if she said no. Here we invited her to New York to publicize her books, and now all she'd get out of it would be work. And some actor would get all the credit and fun."

Actually Jess hadn't thought it sounded like fun at all. She dreaded the thought of having to meet so many strange people and do so much talking. An actor, someone who enjoyed being in the limelight, would be a perfect choice. On the other hand she was not going to be coerced into anything. . . .

Manny walked over to Jess, an ingratiating smile on his face. "What do you think, kid? Would you do it? You'd sure save our lives if you would. And it wouldn't be all work. We'd make sure you saw a lot of New York, wouldn't we, Tory? Tory will get you tickets to some shows, show you the town. You'd only have to work with the actor during the day."

Jess's eyes narrowed as she stared him down. He was the first to drop his eyes, turning finally to Tory.

"No, Manny," said Tory. "I don't think it's fair to ask her to do that. She's a good writer, one of my best. Some actor shouldn't walk off with all the glory. I think the best thing to do would be to send her back

43

to Wyoming and forget the entire publicity campaign."

Bravo, thought Jess, a very Boots Ryan thing to say. Her hero to the rescue—except in this case she didn't really want to be rescued. She didn't fancy being manipulated by these two city slickers, but now that Tory had suggested abandoning the whole thing, she found perversely that she didn't want to return to her cabin quite so soon. Besides, it was as much her fault as theirs. She *had* misrepresented herself. If she had sent the picture and biography he had requested, none of this would have happened.

Her eyes looked over at Tory. And, to be quite honest with herself, to finally meet a man who resembled Boots Ryan—her ideal male—a man she was becoming more attracted to by the moment, and then not stay around long enough to even get to know him. . . . Well, that would be criminal! And if there was even the *slightest* chance they'd replace her with Cody Montana . . .

Jess sauntered over to the chair she had cleared off earlier and sat down, stretching her legs out in front of her. "I think it sounds like fun, TT Thrée," she said, her green eyes gleaming.

Tory ignored the others' looks at her use of TT3. "I thought we agreed on Tory," he said softly.

"It's just that I've thought of you so long as—"

"And I've thought of you as an old cowpoke," he said with a grin. "So I'll start thinking of you as a woman and you start thinking of me as Tory. Okay?" He held out his hand across the desk and she shook it, wryly noting that she had calluses and he did not.

But he did have a nice firm grip. She liked a man with a firm grip. In fact, she liked a man who shook hands with a woman; in her experience men rarely condescended to it.

He held on to her hand for a few moments, then let go of it and turned to Manny. "I still don't feel right about it. We've got a reputable house, and you're suggesting we now pull a scam on the public."

Just what Boots would have said, thought Jess. And she wondered if from now on she'd think of Tory when she wrote about Boots. She also wondered what he'd look like dressed as Boots—with tight-fitting jeans and a shirt unbuttoned to show his chest. She found she was staring at Tory in an unbusinesslike way and quickly dropped her eyes.

"*You* tell the stockholders," Manny was muttering.

"How about a compromise?" suggested Allison. "Forget the talk shows, that might be a bit much. But for the personal appearances in the stores and the pictures in the newspapers, I don't see anything wrong with it. We'd be giving the fans what they want. What they *expect.* I don't see the difference between a phony cowboy in the stores and all the phony Santa Clauses."

"What do you think, Manny?" asked Tory.

Manny had stopped pacing and was standing there, rocking back on his heels. "Yeah—we can cut down on the campaign. Listen, this has been done before anyway. There're precedents."

"And speaking of precedents," said Tory, "I want

it okayed with the legal department. If they say it's all right, well—then we'll go ahead."

Manny was looking greatly relieved when he left the office, and Allison was looking very pleased with herself.

Tory looked at Allison. "Did you find Jess a hotel?"

Allison nodded. "I booked her a suite at the Plaza. It's in a better neighborhood than the Algonquin anyway."

"The Algonquin. Now, I know *that's* American Indian," Jess murmured. "And the Plaza . . . sounds Spanish. I like that."

Allison and Tory looked at each other in confusion.

Tory knocked the ashes out of his pipe and replaced it in the stand. "Okay, Alli, take her over there and get her settled. Incidentally I don't suppose you happen to know of an actor—"

"Sure, I know quite a few who would be good."

"Look, we're not looking for Robert Redford. Some old geezer, a character actor, you know?"

"I know what you have in mind, Tory. In fact, there's an actor in one of my classes who might be perfect."

"What kind of class?" asked Jess.

"Acting."

"You're an actress?" Jess had never met an actress before.

Allison was about to answer when Tory cut in. "If you're around New York long enough, Jess, you'll find that half the women are would-be actresses.

46

Only Alli's too valuable to me here, so I'm not going to allow her to get famous."

"I don't know who you have in your class," said Jess with a grin, "but I personally wouldn't mind Robert Redford."

"He's too well-known," said Allison.

Tory ignored the exchange. "When you've gotten her settled, get hold of some of them and set up appointments for them to come in tomorrow. And no Equity ones, you understand? I don't want this thing going through a union. We'll hold an audition here, right in the office."

"Do I get to sit in on it?" asked Jess.

Tory hesitated, looking at her with narrowed eyes.

"She should, Tory," said Allison. "After all, she's the one who's going to have to work with him."

Tory nodded. "All right, but I have the final say. And remember, we're not picking an actor because he's sexy or you like the way he looks."

Jess looked at him with wide eyes. "As far as I'm concerned, the most important requisite is that he be able to read fast. I'm going to insist he become familiar with all my books."

Tory looked as though he didn't know whether to approve of what she said or disbelieve it. Finally he said a grudging "Right." He looked at Allison. "And have Linda get me two tickets to one of the shows for tonight. Anything in particular you want to see, Jess?"

Jess hadn't the slightest idea what shows were even *on* Broadway. "There's no need for you to entertain me, Mr. Tyler."

"I thought I told you to call me Tory! Look, Jess. I'm not doing it because Manny suggested it. I had planned on entertaining you while you were in town anyway, only I had a little different kind of entertainment in mind for a cowboy."

Jess looked interested. "What kind of entertainment?"

"Never mind! I'd rather see a show than hit the bars anyway."

"Thanks, Tory, but I think I'll pass on it," said Jess. She thought that too much of Tory in one day might be a little overwhelming. If she was this attracted to him in a business office, God only knows what might happen if she was alone with him at night.

Tory looked affronted. "Am I to take that to mean you don't like my company?"

"Not at all," said Jess. "I enjoyed lunch very much, and I thank you for it. I just thought I'd spend this evening walking around the city, getting to know my way around."

Tory looked shocked. "I don't want you walking around the city alone—it's dangerous."

Jess laughed. "If I can walk around the mountains alone, I'm sure I'll be all right in the city. I don't think I'll run into any bears or falling rocks or avalanches, will I?"

Allison was looking concerned. "He's right, Jess. You better do your walking around the city in the daytime. There's plenty of dangers you probably don't run into in Wyoming. And if you *do* go out at night, take a taxi."

"That's a waste of money when I have my own two feet," protested Jess. She had been shocked at the cost of the taxi from the airport.

"While you're in town you're the responsibility of Tanner Books," said Tory in a bossy manner, "and I would very much appreciate it if you'd just do as we suggest."

Jess was appalled at this new aspect of Tory's. Did he think he was some macho man of the West who was going to order her around? If so, he had another thing coming.

"How about a musical," Tory suggested before she had thought of a suitable retort.

Maybe she *would* go out with him that evening. There were a few things she'd like to straighten him out about. She looked down at herself. "Can I go like this?"

Tory frowned. "Is that all you brought with you?"

"That's all I wear. I did bring a change of clothes, but the others are just like these."

"Alli, get her some clothes. It can go as expenses for the promotion."

Jess shook her head. "There's no point in buying clothes I'd never have occasion to wear again. I don't like seeing money thrown away like that."

Tory eyed her thoughtfully. "A miser as well as a recluse, I presume."

Jess matched his glance. "I don't believe in active consumerism, that's all. I limit my spending to just the essentials."

"If people limited their spending to just the essen-

49

tials," countered Tory, "nobody would buy your books."

"I consider books essential," said Jess, "but they could take them out of the library like I do."

"I never met a woman who didn't like dressing up," said Tory, looking totally confused by the whole conversation. "*Or* spending money."

Allison was looking from Tory to Jess, trying to suppress a smile. "Well, I've got to say, you two sure don't have much in common," she observed with amusement.

Tory laughed out loud. "But what a challenge it would be to try and corrupt her," he said to Allison.

"Or to try and reform you," murmured Jess.

"Don't even think about it," he said softly.

"Tory likes living well," observed Allison.

"Living well doesn't necessarily mean—" began Jess.

"Enough!" said Tory, holding his hands up in surrender. "We can argue the relative merits of the simple life versus the good life later."

Allison looked down at Jess. "You can go to the theater like that, Jess. Lots of people wear jeans there these days. Of course, Tory will probably be in a tux. . . ."

"Watch it, Alli," warned Tory with a scowl.

"Well, if you don't mind the way I'm dressed. . . ." Jess was hesitating.

"As long as *you* don't object to the way *I* dress," said Tory.

Jess looked him over. "Couldn't you wear—"

"I don't *own* any," Tory cut in.

"I was going to say *jeans*."

"I *know* what you were going to say."

A man who didn't own jeans? That seemed unfathomable to Jess. And in that case she'd *never* get to see him looking totally like Boots Ryan.

"Oh, Tory, I'm sure you own some jeans," teased Allison.

He raised one brow in her direction. "Have you ever *seen* me in jeans?"

"Well, no."

He spread his hands as thought that confirmed his statement.

"Not even a pair of designer jeans?" Allison persisted.

"You may think I'm pretentious, Alli, but I'm not *that* pretentious." He turned to Jess. "If you'll excuse me now, I have work to do if I want to get out of here in time to take you to the theater. I'll pick you up around eight, and we'll get dinner after the show, all right?"

Jess nodded abstractedly, still bemused by a man who didn't own a pair of jeans.

"On to the Plaza," said Allison, and Jess exited the office wondering what to expect. It sounded more like a hotel in Mexico than one in New York, but if they had Indian restaurants, she guessed anything was possible.

51

CHAPTER FOUR

"Is Mr. Tyler married?" She and Allison were riding in a taxi to the hotel and Jess could no longer control her curiosity about Tory. The cab was speeding up Madison Avenue, winding its way in and out of the traffic while shop after shop vied for Jess's attention. She was more interested in the crowds of people, which never seemed to diminish.

"No." Allison sounded surprised at the question. "Not that there haven't been a few women who thought they had him hooked. Why? Are you interested?"

Jess felt herself flush and kept her face averted. "Not at all. I just wondered how he was free to take me to the theater." She regretted asking now. Allison would probably repeat the conversation to Tory, who would get the misguided impression that she was interested in him personally, which she was not.

"Oh, he's free at the moment as far as I know. Tory's pretty closed-mouthed about his personal life, what there is of it. But if he was seeing someone, she'd probably be calling the office all the time, and I'd hear about it. They usually do."

All she had wanted was a simple yes or no; she really hadn't wanted to hear all about his personal life.

"But I really don't think he's the marrying kind," mused Allison, warming to the subject. "Not like Manny, who's already on his third and swears by marriage. You *never* catch Manny working all hours and weekends."

His *third?* Tory had seemed much more the type to Jess.

"Tory's what I'd have to call a workaholic, you know what I mean? I know he likes women, but he *loves* working. I mean, really loves it!"

"So do I," inserted Jess.

Allison turned wide eyes on her. "Well, I guess you'd have to, sitting all alone all day writing the way you probably do. But I figure you work for money or fame or power or something like that, and it seems to me Tory's already achieved all that to some degree. He could afford to stop working so hard now and just enjoy himself."

"Well, I don't know about Tory, but for me the enjoyment is in the work itself. I don't care about being famous, and just a book a year would bring in enough money to support myself. If for any reason I *don't* work for any period of time, I feel . . . well, incomplete somehow. I really love writing."

"I guess I feel the same way about acting," agreed Allison. "But those are creative things; there's some urge in us that makes us want to do them. But business? I really couldn't get that enthralled about publishing books. Anyway, if you're interested in Tory, I personally think you'd be good for him."

"*Me?* We're complete opposites, Alli, you just said so yourself back at the office." Anyway it wasn't Tory so much as his uncanny resemblance to Boots.

"You know the old saying, Jess: Opposites attract."

Maybe they attract, thought Jess, but they sure couldn't live together. Not that she was looking for someone to live with; she was perfectly happy on her own. "He certainly wasn't at all like what I expected," admitted Jess.

"What did you think he'd be like?"

"Oh . . . much older, dignified—the tweedy type."

Allison laughed. "Then you were both in for a surprise, I guess, although you've got to admit, his was greater."

Jess didn't want to be reminded of it.

"He and Manny are both thirty-four," said Allison. "They started the business really young, practically right out of college. Tory had an inheritance from his grandmother, I think, and they've really made a success of it. And while thirty-four is really young to be so successful, I *do* think that if a man hasn't been married yet by that age, he probably never will be. I tell Tory that, and he just laughs."

"Maybe he isn't interested in marriage, Alli. Did you ever think of that?"

"Of course, I've thought of that, but it isn't natural."

"*I* never want to get married either," confided

Jess. "As far as I'm concerned, living alone is the only way."

Allison gave her an impish grin. "See? You two *do* have something in common after all."

Thirty-four, mused Jess, turning again to look out of the taxi window. She had never been out with anyone so much older than she was. Of course, she had hardly been out at all since college, and then her dates had all been classmates. Robert had been twenty-eight, which she had thought was rather old at the time. Not that tonight could be considered a date; it was strictly business.

The taxi turned west, and Jess noticed a park out the window. "What's that?" she asked Allison.

"Central Park, one of the more scenic spots in the city."

In no time the taxi was nosediving to a stop in front of the Plaza, and they got out, Jess hoisting the backpack onto her shoulders while Allison paid the driver. She looked up at the facade of the building. "It's not Spanish," she noted with surprise.

Allison laughed. "No, but I think you'll like it. It's kind of old-world and charming. And wait until you've had tea at the Palm Court."

Jess couldn't help but notice the elegantly clad women in the lobby of the hotel or the look the desk clerk gave her when she registered. Well, if those people showed up in Rocky Springs dressed New York–style, they'd get looked at too, she thought wryly.

The bellboy offered to carry her backpack, but she assured him she could manage it, and the three of

55

them took an elevator up to her suite. He showed them through the luxurious rooms, furnished with antiques. Jess thought it was a lot of room for just one person; her entire cabin could have fit into the living room, and the bedroom had two double beds, which seemed superfluous. She spent most of the time looking in the door to the bathroom, an expression of anticipation on her face. A real bathtub with hot and cold running water! She sighed at the luxury of it. How delightful not to have to boil water to fill a tub that had to be dragged in from outdoors every time she wanted a bath. She could hardly wait to try it out.

"Come see the view, Jess," Allison called to her from the front of the suite.

Jess dragged herself away from the bathroom and walked over to where Allison stood at the windows. "Great. I thought I'd be looking out at more buildings."

"Central Park is a very expensive view. All I can see out the window of my apartment is an air shaft."

"How big is it?"

"The air shaft?"

Jess chuckled. "No, Central Park."

"Oh, I don't know—miles, I guess. There's a lake and a restaurant, and in the summer they have concerts and operas in the park and Shakespeare and all kinds of things."

"Are people allowed to camp out in there?" Jess had visions of spending a night in a pup tent.

Allison looked at her with horror. "Anyone that foolish would probably be dead in the morning, Jess.

56

Don't even think about it. It's okay to walk in there in the daytime, but stay away from it after dark."

"Are there animals?"

"There's a zoo."

"Well, what's so dangerous?"

"Muggers, for one thing. Look, Jess, I'm not paranoid about the city like some people, but muggings happen every day, and nothing could get me in there at night. At least not to walk around."

Jess couldn't believe so many people would live in a place where they didn't feel safe. "Maybe there should be park rangers," she said, thinking about the Rockies.

"There's police in there," said Allison, "but they can't be everywhere at once." She gave Jess a worried look, then impulsively reached out and hugged her. "Listen, I have to get back to the office now, will you be all right?"

"I'll be fine. I'm going to have a bath."

Allison smiled. "Okay. Have fun tonight, and I'll see you tomorrow at the office."

Alone in the suite, Jess pulled off her boots, then took her backpack into the bedroom and began unpacking. She had brought along an extra pair of jeans, a red flannel shirt, a navy-blue wool sweater, several pairs of cotton pants, and socks. She hung her clothes up in the closet, put her underwear and socks in one of the dresser drawers, then got undressed. Her jeans and shirt were still clean, so she hung them up, but she took her pants and socks into the bathroom to wash out. The hotel had even provided bub-

57

ble bath and shampoo and little bars of soap wrapped in pretty paper.

She spent close to an hour in the tub, letting more hot water run in whenever it started to cool off, and washing her hair three times with the shampoo. Even so, when she was dried off and once again dressed, it was only a little past four, and she had nothing to do until Tory picked her up at seven thirty.

She went to the window and looked out. She could see people going into Central Park and she guessed it was still safe. Unless, of course, those were all muggers going in there to work. She decided she was not going to be scared off by stories. Plenty of people were frightened to hike around the mountains by themselves too. It was just a matter of confidence and knowing how to take care of yourself.

She paused in the lobby to take a look in the window of a boutique. Two silk blouses were tastefully displayed, one in ivory and one in pale green. Maybe she *should* buy something to wear to the theater. She certainly wouldn't want to embarrass Tory by being the only one there in jeans and a flannel shirt.

She went into the shop and asked the saleswoman the price of the silk shirts. When she did a quick calculation in her head and realized she could buy two dozen new flannel shirts for the price of one silk blouse, she decided her wool sweater would do just fine. Anyway she never wore a bra, and that just might be too obvious under a silk blouse. She certainly wouldn't want Tory to get the idea she was trying to entice him.

Outside the fresh air felt good after the steam heat in the hotel. She crossed the street, and at the entrance to the park a man was selling hot dogs. She knew dinner would be late, so she bought four to carry with her in the park. She saw now that more people were heading out of the park than into it, but it didn't deter her. She set off along one of the paths, but it was filled with mothers pushing strollers and people walking dogs and even a few joggers and cyclists, so she soon branched off on her own. Looking back, she could see the top of the Plaza up above the trees, and she knew with her good sense of direction she wasn't likely to get lost.

There were trees and bushes and rock formations, and she felt more at home than she had since arriving in the city. It felt so good to be able to stretch her legs and get some exercise. She walked up and down hills, climbed up rocks, even found the lake, which in her opinion wasn't much of a lake at all. In Wyoming it would be considered barely more than a puddle. But for a city park it wasn't bad at all, and she was glad of its proximity to her hotel.

She realized that she was enjoying herself; in fact, had been enjoying herself almost continuously since her arrival. The trip she had dreaded back in Wyoming had so far turned out to be quite pleasurable. After the first shock of finding out she was a woman, Tanner Books hadn't fired her as a writer, which had been the very worst thing she had envisioned happening. She was getting a chance, all expenses paid, to see what was probably the most famous city in the world. She had met Allison, whom she liked, and

Manny, whom she found amusing. And TT3, of course, who had turned out to be so different from what she had expected. And she had to admit that it was kind of nice after two years of avoiding men to meet one who stirred up her senses again. Not that anything would come of it—nor did she want it to— but it was still nice. Exciting even. She was looking forward to seeing him that night with the same kind of excitement she always felt when embarking on a new book. There was a sense of adventure to it, a sense of exploring the unknown. Which was what she had always liked about the mountains, too, she suddenly realized.

When it began to get dark, she headed back in the direction in which she had come. All around the park the lights of the city were starting to go on, and it was a beautiful sight. When she exited the park at 59th Street she bought two fat hot pretzels to take back to her room to nibble on. She had thought of having tea at the Palm Court in the hotel, but decided she probably wasn't dressed for it. She didn't like tea anyway.

When Jess met Tory in the lobby, he wasn't wearing the tux that Allison had threatened, but was looking extremely handsome in a black houndstooth check sport jacket, black wool slacks, and a white cashmere turtleneck sweater.

Jess, her shining hair falling in waves to below her shoulders, her cheeks pink from a last-minute hot bath she had taken, was wearing clean jeans and her navy-blue sweater, her sheepskin jacket hung over her arm.

Tory smiled as she looked him over. "Do I pass inspection?"

"You look lovely," she told him with a deadpan look, but her green eyes were sparkling.

He lifted an amused brow. "Still trying to get a rise out of me, aren't you? Unlike you backwoods recluses, we New Yorkers have to keep up appearances."

He took her jacket from her and held it while she slipped her arms into the sleeves. She felt herself shiver when his hand brushed her neck as it lifted up her hair to let it fall outside the collar of the jacket. Good grief, the slightest touch of this man, and she nearly went to pieces. She wondered what would happen if he *really* put his hands on her.

"Ready to go?" he asked.

She nodded, and he put her arm through his and led her out of the hotel. A doorman got them a taxi, and minutes later they were dropped off in front of the theater.

"That wasn't much of a trip," said Jess. "We could have walked."

"Tourists walk. Famous authors get driven around town in taxis."

A crowd was in front of the theater and, looking around, Jess saw that Allison had been right. A lot of young people were dressed just like her in jeans and boots, while the older people were more dressed up. She looked at Tory and thought they made an odd pair; he, so impeccably handsome, and she, looking like something right off the farm. He didn't seem to mind though. He was looking down at her, not around checking out the other women as most of the men she had known had the habit of doing.

"We have time for a quick drink if you'd like," he was saying, and she nodded.

She needed something to relax her. She felt tense, keyed up. Being alone with Tory was unsettling. The cab ride, although mercifully brief, had been especially uncomfortable with both of them close together in the backseat.

He took her arm and led her halfway down the block to a bar that seemed to be filled to capacity. People were even standing outside the door with their drinks.

"Theater crowd," he told her. "The bars will be practically empty by seven thirty."

He ordered her a whiskey without asking and a martini for himself. She drank a third of it straight down, and the tenseness magically eased. She wondered if she'd become an alcoholic if she was around Tory long enough, but then dismissed the notion. She recognized sexual tension, and she knew it wouldn't go on forever, or at least she fervently hoped not. Either it would die a natural death from inertia, or something would happen to ease it. And it was that *something* that she kept thinking about.

"A penny for your thoughts?" he was asking her, and Jess almost laughed out loud.

"They're not worth a penny," she said, feeling her face grow warm. She was crowded up next to him behind a group of people at the bar, and every time she moved, even to take a sip of her drink, she brushed against his side. If he *knew* her thoughts, he'd only think her the most inexperienced hick he had ever come across. She was feeling as though she had never been out with a man before, and that was utter nonsense. Just think of him as Boots, she instructed herself, and talk to him like a friend.

"So what happened with the legal department, Tory?" she asked in her best buddy-buddy manner.

He looked perplexed. "The legal department?"

"You know, about hiring an actor?"

"Oh, that. The consensus seems to be we can go ahead, but since lawyers are always reluctant to give a firm answer on anything until they've checked every decision in the last fifty years, we won't really know for sure for a few days. But we're going to go ahead anyway. Time's short, and we might as well get started. That way, if they give us the okay, we're ahead of the game."

Well, that took care of that. Now what should they talk about? "Just think, Tory, if things had worked out the way you wanted, you'd be standing in a western bar now listening to cowboy music."

"I'd far rather be here," he assured her. "And, just to set the record straight, I find this *better* than what I had anticipated."

"That's nice of you to say—"

He put an arm around her shoulder, and *not* in a buddy-buddy manner. "I'm not being nice, Jess. Do you really think I'd rather spend the evening with some old cowboy?"

"It could have been a *young* cowboy."

He tightened his arm. "I much prefer a young women."

The arm was a mistake, she decided. It had been bad enough to be pressed up against him, but now she was practically in his arms. Maybe if they had been alone, it would have been different, but in public, with people all around them, it only made her nervous. And the whiskey wasn't helping all that much.

"Are you this nice to all your authors?" she asked, then wished she hadn't said it. How in the world had she come up with such a fatuous remark? It seemed to smack of the kind of silly flirting she had always avoided.

When he answered, "Only the good-looking ones," she was even sorrier she had said it.

She tried unsuccessfully to move away from him, but that only resulted in her being pressed up against a total stranger. "Listen, Tory. I think there's something I ought to tell you."

He smiled. "You really are an old cowboy disguised as a woman?"

She chuckled. "No."

"I don't think I can take any more surprises today. Anyway the play starts soon, I think we better go."

He was finishing his drink when she said quickly, "It's just that I'm off men."

Jess finished her drink as he got over his choking fit, then he took her arm once again and set off for the theater.

"Did I hear you correctly? Did you say you were *off men?*"

"I'll explain later," said Jess, hurrying into the theater with him and wishing she hadn't even mentioned it. It did sound pretty presumptuous of her. After all, there was no need to warn him off until she was sure he was interested. Maybe he was just being nice to her because she was one of his writers. But she didn't think so. She had a gut feeling he was just as attracted as she was. Then again, it might just be wishful thinking on her part. And her gut feelings had frequently turned out to be wrong in the past. At least where it came to men.

She took her seat next to him and tried to ignore the questioning look in his eyes.

"Off men?" he muttered.

The lights were being dimmed, and the theater was growing silent. "Never mind, Tory, forget I said it."

"No, I'm not going to forget it; you must have said it for a reason."

"Yes, but now I wish I hadn't."

The people seated in front of them turned around with annoyed looks.

"What do you mean, you're off men?"

"I wish she'd just tell him," they could hear a woman behind them murmur, and Jess couldn't stifle a chuckle.

He was still staring at her, waiting for a reply, when the stage lights went up and the audience burst into applause at the realistic set of an artist's studio. Then the star of the show, a well-known actress, ran on stage to answer the phone and the audience once again applauded.

Tory leaned down and whispered in her ear.

"Don't think I'm going to forget about this. I'm going to demand an answer at intermission."

The people in front of them once again turned around with warning looks.

Jess tried to become interested in the play, but it was difficult. It was about a woman artist and a man she met through a personal ad in the newspaper, and Jess knew how it was going to end before it had hardly begun. It was about as interesting as watching a sitcom on TV, which is why she didn't have a set. That and a lack of electricity, of course.

She was conscious of the darkness of the theater, of the closeness of Tory beside her. She moved in her seat, feeling restless, and her leg brushed against his. She left it there and could feel a slight pressure from his, only maybe she was imagining it. Maybe she just wanted to feel it. She stole a glance at him, but he seemed engrossed in the play, laughing at the right parts, enjoying the situation on stage when all she could concentrate on was her own situation.

She moved her arm to put it on the armrest, but found his already there. She shifted toward the other side of her seat, but he was taking her hand and guiding it through his arm so that they could share the armrest, only now his upper arm was gently touching the side of her breast. She caught her breath at the touch, the feeling of warmth radiating through her wool sweater and onto her naked breast beneath.

Get ahold of yourself, Jess ordered herself. What did you think—that you could be celibate for two years and maybe you would just turn to stone? You're human, just as you always were, and he's a damn attractive man, and you're simply reacting the way any normal woman would.

Only she had never considered herself a normal woman. She had always thought of herself as super-human, she realized, as someone who could order her life just the way she wanted—and to hell with human frailties like companionship and love. And sex.

Sure, it was easy enough when she was miles from anywhere and never came into any contact with eligible men—or when she was thrown into daily contact with the most obnoxious of men. And then the first man she met who was slightly different from the others, she immediately fell in love with.

She felt an almost overwhelming desire to move even closer so that her breast would be tight, tight against his arm, but instead, she shifted in her seat, straining away from him, trying to get herself under control. He would think she was crazy if he knew what she was thinking. She was sure he wasn't like her—didn't purposely avoid women for years at a time to prove something or other to himself. He probably didn't notice they were even touching, or else touched women so often, it meant nothing at all to him.

Well, you've got two choices, she told herself, trying to make her mind work in a logical manner. Either you make some excuse and run back home to the mountains where it's safe, or you admit you're human and go with it. It's not love, it couldn't be love, and love is really the only danger. Love is what makes you end up tied down to some man and giving up your own life for his. You don't know him well enough for it to be love, it's just plain lust, so your other choice is to stick around for a while and see what comes of it, and if it's an affair while you're in town, well, you can live with that.

And maybe he's not interested anyway. So what if he said you were beautiful and fascinating? That was a New Yorker talking, someone who knows his way around women, has a way with words. It probably doesn't mean a thing. And to him it probably *is* business, taking the visiting author out on the town.

The darkness of the overheated theater began to combine with the whiskey; she remembered she had got up very early that morning after a sleepless night, and then taken a long flight, and suddenly all her mind was concerned with was just staying awake and not embarrassing Tory by falling asleep in the theater.

Just as her head was beginning to nod, there was a burst of applause and the house lights went up, and all Jess was hoping was that the play was over and now they would be able to get some air.

"You want to go out to the lobby and get a drink?" he was asking her, and she looked around and saw that not everyone was leaving; the play obviously had another act.

"No, thanks. That one was starting to put me to sleep," she confessed, "but I'll go out with you if you want one."

He shook his head. "We can just stay here and talk."

"But I wouldn't mind getting some air and

stretching my legs," she said quickly, hoping he wouldn't remember what they had been talking about just before the play began.

No such luck. As soon as they were in front of the theater, he said, "Now, Jess Haggerty, I'd like to know just what you meant by that remark."

She turned innocent eyes to his. "What remark, TT Three?"

He ignored the TT3. "About your being off men. Was that supposed to be a warning?"

If she could just learn to keep her big mouth shut things like this wouldn't happen. How *could* she have said such a dumb thing. "No, it wasn't meant as a warning. Why should you need a warning?" Why, indeed. And why hadn't she thought of that before she said it? she wondered.

He put both hands on her shoulders and looked down at her, his dark eyes serious. Her eyes dropped to the pavement, seemingly finding it fascinating.

"Let's not play games, Jess. I'm not ashamed to admit when I'm attracted to a woman, and I think it's pretty obvious I'm attracted to you. I hoped it was mutual. But then you threw out that remark, and now I don't know *what* to think."

Jess let out a sigh of relief. He *was* attracted to her, which meant she hadn't made such a complete fool of herself after all.

He seemed to be waiting for a reply which wasn't forthcoming. "Well?" he prodded her. "What is it? Do you have a husband stashed away back in Wyoming? A jealous boyfriend? But in that case I guess you wouldn't say you were off men. Do you hate men? Is that it?"

The fact that he really was interested in her gave her back her confidence. She looked up at him and shrugged. "I just meant what I said: I'm off men. I don't hate them, I just don't have much use for them."

"Not for *anything*?"

"Not lately anyway," she said somewhat evasively. She really didn't think this was the time or place to go into it. The crowd was beginning to go back inside the theater, and she glanced that way rather pointedly, hoping he'd get the message.

He took her arm and they returned to their seats, but as soon as they were seated, he said, "How long has it been since you've been out with a man?"

"Two years," she said, slipping out of her jacket and making herself comfortable. She hoped the second act wouldn't last as long as the first.

"*Two years?*" His incredulous tone brought stares from the people seated in front of them.

"Well what did you think I meant, that I was off them this week?"

"But *two years?* You really are a recluse!"

"I told you I was."

"Well, we'll have to do something about that," he said softly, but not so softly that several of the people around them didn't start to say "Shush." The house lights were now going down and the second act starting.

Jess made a brief effort to watch the second act, but ten minutes into it she was sound asleep, and the next thing she knew, Tory was gently shaking her shoulder and she saw that the lights were back on and everyone was leaving.

"I won't ask you how you liked the play," he said as they were walking up the aisle.

"I'm really sorry. It's just that it's been a long day."

"I should have realized that. Are you too tired for dinner?"

Jess was never too tired for dinner and said so.

"Good. Then we can continue our interesting discussion."

Jess debated forgoing dinner to avoid the discussion, but hunger pangs won out.

CHAPTER FIVE

Onde's was dimly lighted; the restaurant had a general air of intimacy about it, and a group was playing soft music for the people on the dance floor. Jess followed the waiter to a corner table—a bud vase with a single pink rose gracing its center—and was seated next to Tory. Their knees touched beneath the small table, and she smiled to herself at the romantic setting he had brought her to. She wanted only to look at Tory, but instead glanced around at the other patrons.

"I'm not dressed for this place," she said with a sigh.

"They'll just think you're *somebody,*" he said, then added, "and you are."

"A writer of westerns! Big deal!" said Jess. If nobody in Rocky Springs thought she was somebody, surely no one in this big city would.

"Don't underestimate your talent," said Tory. "Do you have any idea how many people think of themselves as writers but have never written a word? Or how many writers spend years sending out manuscripts and never get anything but rejections? You're special, Jess—a genuinely successful writer. Less than ten percent of writers can even support themselves on their writing, and yet, you're doing just that. Of course, being a miser might have *something* to do with it."

Jess laughed. "You had to put that qualifier on at the end, didn't you?"

He chuckled. "I didn't want you to get so puffed up you wouldn't even eat dinner with a nobody like me. Are you hungry?"

"Starved."

"Well, it's been a long time since lunch."

Jess agreed with him, ignoring the fact that since then she'd consumed four hot dogs, to say nothing of the hot pretzels.

"Their steaks are excellent."

"Fine," she agreed, noticing the young couple at the next table who were obviously in love and having trouble keeping their hands off each other.

"Baked potatoes, asparagus, red wine?"

She nodded in agreement, and he called the waiter and placed their order. Then he stood up and reached for her hand. "While we wait for our food, let's dance."

Jess hadn't danced in years; she didn't even know if she remembered how, but the music was slow, the kind you barely had to move to, so she thought she could manage. And she certainly wasn't going to turn down the opportunity of being in Tory's arms.

He pulled her close to him on the dance floor, both of his arms going around her back, so that it was more of an embrace than a dance position, but Jess didn't mind. She fitted her body to his and rested her head alongside his shoulder, then moved to the music as he was doing, although it felt more like she was moving to some music deep inside herself.

She pressed against him as his hard thighs guided her legs and one of his hands moved up and down her back, stirring feelings in her long dormant. She had never danced with Robert and couldn't remember dancing anything but disco with Mark, which was a shame when she thought about it. Dancing was certainly a nice way to get close to someone you liked. And she was liking Tory more by the minute.

"You're going braless, I see," he murmured, breaking into Jess's thoughts and causing her to move her head back and look up at him.

"I don't even *own* a bra," she informed him. "I stopped buying them years ago. I think they're a waste of money—not that it's any of your business."

"I wasn't complaining," he assured her, pressing her head back against his shoulder. "Just noting a fact."

"And the fact is," she said, her voice slightly muffled, "I only buy essentials, and—"

"Frugality does have its advantages," he said, cutting in on her diatribe, and Jess subsided.

He moved his lips against her hair and pulled her even closer, if that was possible, and Jess luxuriated in the feeling of once again being in a man's arms. How could she have forgotten how good it felt? she wondered, although her body obviously hadn't forgotten. If only it could stay like this, but it never did. Eventually the man's ego got in the way, and then

74

the good feelings were all over—and she found that it was only herself she could really count on. Really trust. And what a shame, because it was so nice.

"I think you're just as attracted as I am," he whispered in her ear, his breath warm on her skin.

"Oh, I'm attracted," she admitted. "But that's all."

"That's enough."

"Not for me, it isn't!"

Now he was the one to back off and look down at her while they danced. "What do you want, undying love on a first date?"

"This isn't a date," insisted Jess.

"That doesn't answer my question."

She met his eyes. "No. At least *attraction* is honest. I don't even believe in undying love."

He shook his head. "Twenty-five and already so cynical."

"I'm a fast learner."

"Well, you'll just have to unlearn it."

"And if I don't want to?"

He stopped dancing and took her hand. "Let's go back and see if our wine's there yet. There's something unromantic about arguing on the dance floor."

"And so you've decided to ply me with liquor instead?" asked Jess, a look of mischief in her eyes.

"That might cross my mind if you were just an average woman, but someone who can consume whiskey like you—I just don't think it would work."

"You're right, it wouldn't."

He held her chair for her. "Just a hard-drinking, straight-talking gal of the West, right?"

75

"Right."

"And no amount of romantic talk, soft lights, seductive music, or wine would make even a dent in you, am I right?"

"You could always give it a try," teased Jess.

He laughed. "I just gave it a try and I struck out. However, if you'd care to start over," he said, standing up, "may I have the pleasure of this dance?"

Jess smiled up at him. "Why don't we eat first?" She could see the waiter approaching with their food, and it would be a shame to let a good meal like that get cold.

He sat down shaking his head. "You know, Jess, if you haven't been successful with men in the past, it just might have something to do with your attitude. Did you ever think of that?"

"What's the matter with my attitude?"

"Well, it's hardly conducive to romance."

"My attitude wasn't always like that."

"It is now."

"That's because *now* I'm off men."

Tory waited until the waiter had set their plates in front of them, then said, "I think you're just afraid of letting go, losing control. Sex can be a very beautiful thing—"

"It's not sex I don't like, Tory. It's *men*!"

The couple at the next table took their eyes off each other and focused them on Jess and Tory, making Jess wish she'd spoken in a lower voice.

"Well, unless you're gay, which I have trouble believing—"

"I'm not gay," Jess muttered.

"Oh, you know what *gay* means, living way out there in the middle of nowhere?"

"We *do* get news of the world on occasion," retorted Jess, once more raising her voice.

"Well, if you're not gay, and you don't like men, I hope you're enjoying your celibacy."

The neighboring couple now looked thoroughly engrossed in their eavesdropping. Well, let them listen, thought Jess; maybe they'll learn something.

"It's not something you enjoy," she informed him. "It's a passive condition, not an active one."

"And quite the rage these days, I understand."

Jess looked at him in annoyance. "What do you mean, the rage?"

"The so-called new celibacy has become quite popular; there are books and articles on it all over the place. Or didn't that news of the world reach Rocky Springs yet?"

"Are you making fun of me?" asked Jess.

He gave her a wicked smile. "Did you think you were the only one?"

Actually she had thought just that. The idea of being part of some popular movement revolted her. "I never really thought about it at all. I just decided to do without men, and that was the natural outcome."

"You're not eating your steak."

"That's because you're not giving me a chance!"

Jess started to eat, and the couple next to them went back to their own conversation, clearly disappointed the entertainment was at an end.

Tory poured them both some wine. "What happened? Did the great love of your life dump you?"

The steak was rare and delicious, and Jess hated to swallow it as fast as she was forced to do in order to answer his unwanted questions. "*Both* of them did."

"*Both?*" he asked. "You're only supposed to have *one* great love of your life. As a writer, you should know that."

"Well, I had two."

"And both of them dumped you?"

"What is it with you, Tory? Every time we eat, you want my life story. Can't I just finish this steak in peace?" And why did she always find herself saying the worst possible thing to him? Here she was, attracted to the man, and now she had given him the idea every other man in the world found her so undesirable, he ended up dumping her.

"Didn't you ever learn how to conduct a conversation while you dined?"

"No! Out in Wyoming we concentrate on our food —rather like savages, I'm sure you'd say."

"I wouldn't have said that."

Jess banged her fork down on her plate. "Will you please just let me eat?"

"Go ahead, don't let me stop you. I'll do all the talking. I don't have any trouble doing two things at once." As if to prove his point, he took a bite of his steak. "The steaks are good, aren't they? No, you don't have to answer that, I can see you're enjoying it. And try some of that wine, it might have a mellowing effect on you."

"Tory!" she warned him.

"Don't let me interrupt your eating, Jess; you're doing fine. I've rarely seen a healthier appetite on a woman *or* a man. Of course, some people would probably point out that you're no doubt sublimating other appetites in your appetite for food, but I wouldn't even think such a thing. It's quite possible to enjoy good food *and* good sex, I believe."

Jess sighed and took a drink of her wine. She'd never been much of a wine drinker, but this was good. Tasty. She'd have to buy herself some wine to keep in the cabin when she got back. But as for Tory . . .

"Would you mind not talking about sex while we eat?" she asked him, and once more caught the attention of the nearby couple.

"Does it upset you? Make you lose your appetite? I've never eaten with a celibate before, at least not to my knowledge. Does the thought of sex make you ill?"

Jess gave him a look of outrage, then the humor in the situation struck her, and she started to laugh. "What are you trying to do to me?" she finally managed to say.

"Get to know you."

She glanced over at the spellbound couple and then back at Tory. "Is there never any privacy in New York?"

"We could always go to my place."

She gave him a doubtful look.

"Are you afraid I'd try to seduce you?"

"No, I don't think that."

"Then you're very naive," he said, his eyes warm on her.

"Tory, I'm tired. I just want to finish dinner and go home." Which was true. She also wanted some time to think before this escalated any further.

"Tomorrow night I'll fix you dinner at my place," he said with a smile.

"And try to seduce me?"

"Maybe I'll let *you* try to seduce *me*."

"And if I don't try?"

His smile was confident. "You will after you've tasted my cooking."

"Tory, I'm not *that* interested in food."

"I was hoping you were that interested in me."

"You know, Tory, all this is is a physical attraction," she told him matter-of-factly.

"That's the best kind."

Jess gave him a long look then went back to her food and finished it quickly. She settled back in her chair while Tory poured her some more wine. She really was tired, too tired even to think straight or best TT3 at any argument. She would have a little more wine, maybe some dessert, if he didn't make an issue out of her wanting more to eat, and then she'd like nothing better than to go back to the hotel and get to bed. Alone. If she was going to get together with Tory, it wouldn't be tonight. She'd be far too tired even to enjoy it, and she had a feeling that with Tory it would be something to be enjoyed.

"What are you smiling about?" he asked her.

"Nothing."

"Thinking about tomorrow night?"

She shook her head at his persistence. "No, I was thinking about tonight. And how tired I am. And whether you'd put up a big fuss if I wanted some dessert."

He put his hand over hers on the table. "You can have anything you want, Jess."

"Chocolate cake," she said, having decided on the spot.

"Romance might be alive and well, but it certainly doesn't reside in Wyoming," he muttered as he summoned the waiter to their table.

"I don't notice *you* passing up chocolate cake," countered Jess after he had ordered two.

"All right, you win. Now do you think we can get through the rest of the evening without arguing? We'll eat our dessert, have a cup of coffee, one last dance, and then I'll see you home."

Jess didn't know about the dance. Her resistance was low at the moment, and one more time in his arms and she might be changing her mind about going to his place.

They ate the cake in silence, then when he stood and reached for her hand, she decided one more time wasn't going to hurt anything, and once more let herself be pulled into his arms on the dance floor.

This time he didn't say anything, just held her close, so close that she felt the warmth of his body spreading through hers. Or maybe it was both of them; she couldn't tell anymore.

She was sorry when the music ended and he pulled away to smile down at her. She had felt as if she could stay all night like that, held tightly in his arms and feeling wanted.

When they were riding in the cab to her hotel, he put his arm around her, and she rested her head on his shoulder, feeling sleepy and peaceful and content.

When the cab stopped in front of the hotel, she turned to Tory and said, "Thank you for the lovely evening."

"I'll see you to your door."

"That's not necessary, Tory."

"I *want* to see you to your door."

"Tory," she began, but then saw they had the cab driver's complete attention, and she refused to provide any more entertainment for strangers that evening. She got out of the cab with Tory following her.

"I just want to see that you get safely inside," he said to her.

She didn't even bother telling him that she was used to taking care of herself. Anyway she wasn't that eager to bring the night to an end.

She opened the door to her room and reached inside to switch on the light, then turned to thank him once again for the evening. Before she could even open her mouth to speak, he leaned down and closed his mouth over hers, and then all she knew was the sweet sensation of him kissing her and feeling as if she were drowning in his kiss. Her eyes closed, and she reached out to put her arms around his neck, molding her body to his as she had done on the dance floor. Only now there was no pretense of dancing as they embraced.

When his hand reached to cup her breast, she

shivered at her quick response, feeling her nipple become erect beneath his skillful fingers. She wanted him then, wanted him more than she could ever remember wanting a man, and she wouldn't have resisted if he had pushed her inside the room and closed the door behind them.

His fingers slowly revolved around her taut nipple as his other moved down to pull her hips tightly against his. She sighed, opening her mouth, and his tongue moved inside to duel with her own, sending waves of desire over her that left her trembling. When he moved his hand up under her sweater to cup one naked breast, she pressed hard against him, wanting more, wanting everything he had to give. They stood there for long moments as their tongues explored unfamiliar mouths and his hands made her body feel like pure sensation. She felt stunned by how quickly he had aroused her passion; it had never happened that way with Mark or Robert. And then he broke the kiss, and she was sure he was going to take her inside the room, but his hand dropped to his side and he said a soft "Good night, Jess" to her, leaving her standing with her mouth practically open and her knees feeling weak.

He reached out and gently smoothed the hair back from her face. "You're lovely, do you know that? And very warm and responsive. Celibacy doesn't suit you, darling."

"I thought it did," she murmured, her eyes clinging to his.

"You were wrong." He leaned down and kissed

her briefly on the lips. "Good night. I'll see you in the morning."

"Good night, Tory."

"And remember, I'm looking forward to being seduced tomorrow night." He turned and walked down toward the elevator bank before she could think of a reply.

By the time she had washed her face and brushed her teeth, her mind was able to manage some coherent thoughts. She pulled down the bedspread and slipped under the covers nude, pajamas being another item she didn't consider essential.

What was she going to do with Mr. Torrance Tyler III? she asked herself as she tried to get comfortable on the too soft mattress. Or more important, what did she want to do with him? Well, what she wanted to do seemed fairly obvious from her strong reaction to the encounter outside the door. On the other hand Tory seemed far more experienced than the men she had previously known, and no doubt knew just what to do to get a woman feeling more physical than perhaps she cared to feel.

She shifted from her back onto her side, but it didn't help. The middle part of her still sunk down in the mattress, making her feel uncomfortable. Sleeping like that just couldn't be healthy.

And maybe celibacy wasn't healthy either. No doubt if she had made the acquaintance of a single man or two in Rocky Springs—provided there was such a thing—and had been in the habit of having occasional male companionship, she wouldn't have fallen so hard for the first presentable man to come her way. Which was an understatement, though; Tory was far more than just presentable. Even without the advantages of his Boots Ryan looks, he was intelligent, well-read, fun to be with, sexy as they come, and she enjoyed sparring with his quick wit.

But what was the point of a brief affair with her publisher while she was visiting the city? Brief affairs weren't really her style, and she'd end up returning to Wyoming probably missing the man—and definitely missing the sex. Then what was she to do? It was for darn sure nothing could ever come of it. Nothing serious. Well, maybe serious if you already considered that she was halfway to falling in love already, but nothing *lasting.* There was no way she'd ever live in New York or any city, and she couldn't quite picture Tory running his publishing business from a cabin in the mountains. A cabin sans electricity and telephone and all the other amenities required for running a business.

She rolled onto her stomach and immediately felt the discomfort in the small of her back where it was being bent in an unnatural position. She tried her other side.

I guess there's no use even speculating about it, she finally realized. *Because no matter what great advice I give myself tonight, when he's not around, will probably mean exactly zero when I'm over at his place tomorrow night for the big seduction scene. I already know how I react to him; that's not likely to change overnight.*

With a sigh she reached out and turned on the bedside lamp. She got up and briefly tried the other bed, but it was just as soft. Pulling the blankets off the bed, she arranged a bedroll on the floor and curled up happily, feeling far more at home.

What a terrible waste of money, she mused. *They get me an expensive hotel suite with two beds, and I could just have well slept in a corner of their office.*

But then I would have missed out on the bathtub was her last thought before finally succumbing to sleep.

CHAPTER SIX

Jess always awakened at dawn, and her inner mechanism seemed to be working despite the time change: she was up in time to see a glorious sunrise behind the buildings to the east of Central Park. She put the blankets back on the bed, showered, dressed, then took an hour's brisk hike through the park, surprised to see so many joggers up so early.

She walked to Tanner Books, and on the way stopped for a big breakfast in a coffee shop. It was just after nine when she arrived at the office, and Linda waved her in the direction of Tory's office.

"Go on in, Jess. I think he's waiting for you."

What could have been an awkward moment wasn't. Tory, except for a warm smile, was all business, and Jess sat down and relaxed in the chair after returning his smile.

"Get a good night's sleep?" he asked her.

"Yes, thanks," she replied, which had been true once she had replaced the bed with the floor.

She was wearing her green flannel shirt that brought out the green in her eyes. "You look good," he said.

"So do you." As usual he looked like a fashion plate; he was wearing a three-piece suit of gray flannel with a pale lavender shirt. Once, Jess would have thought lavender would be a silly color on a man, but on Tory it looked great. She felt like going around his desk and giving him a big kiss, but decided that kind of behavior was probably inappropriate in an office.

"The auditions can begin any time you're ready," he told her. "Alli's got a few actors waiting in her office already. Any questions before we start?"

"What exactly will they do when they come in?"

"It won't be like a regular audition, not that you're probably familiar with those. I'll ask them about themselves, where they're from, background information, that kind of thing, and meanwhile we can see what they look like, how well they speak, if they can do a western accent."

"We don't have accents," Jess informed him. "You're the ones with accents."

Tory gave a bark of laughter. "I won't debate that with you now, but you'll at least concede you speak more slowly, right?"

She had to agree with that. Most New Yorkers spoke so fast, she could barely understand them. "Will I be able to question them?" she asked.

"Sure, ask whatever you want. As Alli pointed out, you're the one who's going to have to work with him. And I guess that's another thing we have to do today—work out a schedule for you and the actor. We don't have all that much time. Do you think you could train him in a week?"

"If he's smart enough and a fast reader," she said,

thinking she'd have to remember to get copies of her books from Tory for the actor to read through.

"Hi, Jess," said Allison, poking her head in the door. "Are you two ready for the first one?"

Tory looked at Jess, who nodded. "Bring him in, Alli."

The young man who followed Allison into the office was a surprise to Jess, since he was sporting a full black beard and a mustache reminiscent of a Mexican bandit. He was a possibility though. She knew plenty of men in Wyoming who had beards and mustaches, and he *was* good-looking.

When she was introduced to him as the person he might be working with, his eyes flicked suggestively over her body in a way she didn't care for, but she decided if she was businesslike with him, he would probably follow suit. Particularly if he wanted the job badly enough.

He was dressed in skintight jeans and a black turtleneck sweater, and Jess could easily picture him in boots and a cowboy hat, which is what she was sure Tory would insist on. She'd probably have to restrain him from insisting on spurs and a holster.

As soon as Tory asked the young man to tell them something about himself, and he said his name was Vinnie and he was from the Bronx, Jess had to fight herself to keep from laughing. She had assumed actors would have classes in speech, but this one had evidently either missed the class or flunked it. His New York accent was so strong she was sure he'd be condemned to gangster roles because he wouldn't be much good at anything else. His grammar, also, left

89

a lot to be desired, and Jess cringed at the thought of him playing the role of a writer.

She thought perhaps she was the only one aware of the accent, but then Tory asked Vinnie if he would do a western accent for them, and the actor immediately launched into a terrible imitation of John Wayne. At least Jess thought it was supposed to be John Wayne; it sounded more to her like Humphrey Bogart doing an imitation of John Wayne and failing miserably.

Tory looked over at Allison with a questioning glance.

"Listen, Vinnie," said Allison, "that's a little too Wayne, if you know what I mean. How about just straight western?"

Vinnie gave it another try, but it was still John Wayne as far as Jess was concerned, and she caught Tory's eye and gave an imperceptible shake of her head.

Tory thanked the actor and dismissed him. "The accent could probably be worked on, Jess. I liked his looks, and there's a certain roughness about him that would work."

Jess was adamant. "I don't think he'd get the accent in just a week, and he's going to have enough to learn without learning to speak at the same time. And I'm not a speech teacher, Tory."

"She's right, Tory. Just reading the books would take Vinnie the whole week," said Allison. "He's a good friend, though, and I wanted to give him a shot at it. He's also a good actor in the right parts."

"Also one of your boyfriends?" asked Tory.

Allison ignored the question and brought in the next actor. Jess thought he was much too good-looking, rather young, and a little effeminate, but didn't object out loud to him since Tory also thought him unsuitable and she wanted to save her vetoes for when she needed them. She didn't want Tory to be able to say later on that she had objected to all of them.

After that there was a Puerto Rican actor—and why Allison had invited him Jess couldn't figure out because as far as she knew there were no Puerto Ricans in Wyoming. Now, an Indian—*that* might be interesting.

Then Jack Sheppard walked in and made himself right at home. He dumped a pile of books off the other leather chair, settled himself in it, then took out a pouch of tobacco and began to roll a cigarette. He was dressed to fit the part too—in worn jeans and a flannel shirt that looked very much like Jess's, only Jack's was brown. He even had a bola around his neck with a silver fastener.

"The name's Jack Sheppard," he said, looking up at them, "and I've played a lot of cowboy roles." He went on to list the roles he had played, a seemingly endless list, but didn't name anything Jess could ever remember seeing.

After that he began telling them a series of anecdotes about life in the Old West, spinning them out, inserting jokes that he laughed at himself, and getting quite a few laughs from the occupants in the room. He scratched his grizzled head, rubbed his bristly jaw, knocked imaginary dirt off his boots, and, if he had had a .45, Jess was sure he would have done his fast draw for their enjoyment.

Jess could see that Tory was enthralled by the man and was sure Jack was just what he had had in mind. Probably he was just the way he had pictured *her*. But to her he was more a caricature of what a western writer should be than the reality. And she was awfully afraid he'd bore her to death with all his talk.

When she heard him assure Tory he was a quick study and a speed-reader, Jess figured she was in trouble. But when he was finally dismissed, she didn't say anything, hoping someone else would come along who would be more suitable.

Tory was all for hiring him on the spot and not seeing the rest of the actors, but Allison said there was only one more, and it was only fair to interview him.

When he came in, Jess judged him to be in his early thirties, and her first thought was that he looked more like an accountant or a teacher than an actor, but then she supposed there had to be actors who could play the parts of accountants and teachers. He was rather soft-looking, with a rounded face and the beginnings of a paunch. Unlike the others, who had all been wearing jeans, Philip Bly was neatly attired in a blue suit and tie, and he shook hands with Jess when introduced.

He told them he was originally from Wisconsin, and as far as Jess could tell he didn't have any more of an accent than she did. He had studied drama at Northwestern University and gave them the usual actor's résumé. When he was finished, and Tory didn't speak up to ask a single question, Jess, who had been impressed with his serious way of speaking, decided she'd do the questioning.

"Do you like to read, Mr. Bly?" she asked him.

He looked at her and smiled, a look of intelligence in his brown eyes behind the rimless glasses he wore. "I understand this has to do with westerns," he replied, "and I can't recall ever reading one. I'm a mystery buff myself."

Jess also liked reading mysteries, and she questioned him for a while on which authors he preferred, whether he liked police or detective or psychological thrillers the best, and he was so knowledgeable, she got caught up in the conversation and didn't notice for a while the look of impatience on Tory's face.

"Thank you for coming in," Tory said, finally breaking into the conversation, which Jess thought was exceedingly rude.

"I'd like to ask him a few more questions if you don't mind, Tory," she said sharply.

Tory looked like he did mind, but subsided into silence for the moment.

"Have you ever tried writing yourself, Mr. Bly?" she asked him.

"Actually I've been doing more writing than acting lately," he admitted. "Although I could sure use an acting job."

"What kind of things?"

"Plays. It's really the theater I'm interested in, but I find I like writing every bit as much as acting."

Jess looked over at Tory to signal she was through,

93

and Tory quickly dismissed the actor with his thanks for coming in.

When the three of them were alone in the office, a beaming Tory looked at Allison. "Well, what do you think, Alli? Do you agree with me about Jack?"

Allison shrugged. "I knew he'd be just what you had in mind, Tory, being as he's almost exactly the way you pictured Jess before you met her."

Tory leaned back in his chair and ran his fingers through his hair. "Yeah, he was a real character, wasn't he? I can just picture him sitting around a campfire—"

"But not in front of a typewriter," Jess said pointedly, interrupting Tory's musings.

He looked annoyed. "Look, this is public relations; we've got to have the right package."

"If you like him so much, you can take him to that western bar you told me about. Personally, I liked Philip Bly."

Tory spread his hands. "But he was so . . . so . . . innocuous. Like a professor, or a—"

"Writer?" she asked.

"Listen, Jess. A lot of writers are real characters. Like Hemingway."

Jess shook her head. "I think most writers are educated, serious people, not old characters who hang around campfires. Plus, Philip *reads*."

"Mysteries. What help is that?"

"I think it's a great help. I read mysteries myself, and they're genre books, just like westerns. If he knows how a mystery is constructed, westerns will be a piece of cake to him. And he writes too. I think he's perfect, Tory, and personally I found Jack Sheppard a bore!"

"He *is* boring," interjected Allison. "He never shuts up in class."

"Which means he would be great on the talk shows," argued Tory.

Allison looked at him. "I thought we were forgetting about the talk shows."

"Look," said Jess, "I don't much like the idea of some easterner's idea of a cowboy impersonating me all over town. Philip looked like a writer, and I like that."

"If we're not going to use a cowboy, we might as well use *you*," said Tory.

"He's just as much a cowboy as Jack is," said Jess. "I think you're forgetting they're both actors. Put him in the right clothes, and he'll be fine."

Tory looked displeased. "I see you didn't jump at the chance to play yourself."

"I always *dreaded* the thought of playing myself. I'm no good talking to people I don't know, and I'd rather be anonymous."

"Are you afraid frenzied fans might storm that citadel up there in the mountains and interfere with your hermit's life?"

He could certainly be obnoxious without half trying, Jess thought, her anger coming to the surface. "Maybe I'm afraid I'll turn into one of you slick New Yorkers who has to take a cab everywhere and parties all night!"

Allison jumped in like a referee. "Okay, okay, let's

knock it off, both of you. Fighting isn't going to get us anywhere."

Tory gave an audible sigh. "All right, Alli, why don't you give us your opinion?"

"Personally I liked Vinnie," she said, and they both groaned. "No, seriously, I think Jess has a point. I know what *you* were expecting Jess Haggerty to be, but I always figured he'd be more like Philip. Most of our writers are, you know."

"I had my heart set on a real character," said Tory, clearly disappointed that they weren't in agreement with him.

"Yes, well I had *you* pictured a lot differently too," said Jess sharply, "and I'm not making a fuss that you don't look like my stereotype of the man of publishing."

"What do you mean?" Tory demanded to know.

Allison laughed. "Jess had you pictured as a dignified gentleman, Tory. Can you believe it?"

He looked from one to the other with no trace of humor on his face. "I *am* a dignified gentleman."

Allison started to laugh and Jess joined in.

"Okay, I give in," he said at last. "Call him and set up a schedule, Alli. How many hours a day do you think you can work with him, Jess?"

"I'm willing to work night and day if you want."

Tory didn't look too pleased by her generous offer. "Days will do; we want you to enjoy yourself at night."

Knowing exactly what he meant by "enjoying herself at night," Jess could feel herself blushing.

Allison looked at Jess and then at Tory. "By the

way, did you two enjoy yourselves last night? How was the play?"

"Don't look at Jess—she slept through it."

"It was hot in the theater and the play was boring," said Jess.

"*I* managed to stay awake."

"*You* hadn't been up since dawn."

"I wasn't aware you knew what time I get up in the morning."

"I'll bet it isn't dawn!"

Manny walked into the office, a big grin on his face. "Hey, I saw some old guy leave the office who would be perfect. Did you hire him?"

Tory groaned. "Where were you when I needed you, Manny?"

"Right in my office. Listen, we have a business lunch with the attorneys. You coming?"

"I'll be with you in five minutes," Tory told him, then turned to Allison. "How about taking Jess to lunch, Alli? But don't let her eat too much; I'm cooking dinner for her tonight."

Allison looked amazed. "*You're* cooking?"

"Don't you give me a hard time too, Alli. Just give Jess my address." He turned to Jess. "And I'll see you around eight. And take a taxi, understand?"

"You sure eat dinner late in this town," muttered Jess, thinking she was going to eat an enormous lunch to tide her over.

Tory waved his hands. "Out, both of you, out!"

"I know just the place," Allison said as they left the office, "and I never can afford to eat there on my own. But since this is *business* . . ."

CHAPTER SEVEN

The apartment building in the East Thirties looked new and expensive. It even had a doorman. She had been checked out by the doorman; he was probably trying to make sure if she was dangerous or not, she supposed. She passed the test—just barely, Jess thought—and headed for the elevator. She pushed the button marked *14* and as the elevator began to climb she wondered if the butterflies in her stomach were due to thoughts of Tory or the elevator's motion.

She watched the numbers on the panel as one by one they lighted up, then finally stopped at fourteen, and the door opened quietly. She turned to her right and walked down a carpeted hallway, scanning the letters on the doors. When she realized she was going in the wrong direction, she turned back. Which is really what she wanted to do—turn back. Back to her hotel, back to Wyoming. What was she doing going to the apartment of practically a total stranger, *knowing* she was going to be in for some kind of seduction scene? She could still turn back, call him from the hotel, and plead illness. She wasn't Boots

Ryan; she could occasionally get away with acting cowardly, couldn't she?

She knocked on the door of 14-E, and it opened almost immediately. His dark hair looked wind-blown even indoors. A light blue crewneck sweater topped faded jeans, then farther down the leather moccasins—worn without socks. He stood there with his hands tightly jammed into his pockets as a slow smile formed on his face. A stranger and yet not a stranger.

The semistranger spoke. "What's the matter, Jess? You look like you're going to see the dentist. Don't worry. I'm really a very good cook."

He moved aside as she stepped past him into the entry hall. She felt nervous, unsure of how to act. She took off her jacket and handed it to him, then watched as he hung it in an overly crowded hall closet. She glimpsed coats, a black umbrella, suit-cases on the shelf, and then the door was closed and he was facing her again.

"It wasn't the cooking I was worried about," said Jess, watching as his smile widened. This constant smiling of his wasn't doing anything to allay her unease.

Laughter was glinting in his eyes. "You mean to say the indomitable woman of the wilderness is wor-ried about having dinner alone in a man's apart-ment?" He put his hands on her shoulders, moving his thumbs back and forth against the soft flannel, sending shivers right down her back.

She took a step back, and his arms dropped to his sides. "If I were alone, I wouldn't be worried," she murmured. "And I thought you didn't own a pair of jeans?"

"I lied. Do you mind?"

"In this case, no. You look much less formidable in jeans." And much more familiar to Jess, who was used to seeing men in jeans, not three-piece suits.

He looked pleased. "Does that mean you usually think of me as formidable?"

"You can be formidable, Tory."

"I'm glad to hear it. To tell the truth, I've found *you* a bit formidable at times."

"*Me?*" She liked the sound of it, but didn't believe it.

"Well, a woman who can't be bribed with clothes or jewels . . ."

Jess laughed. "You just haven't found the right bribe yet. Try a new Winchester or some fishing gear or even a shortwave radio."

He took her hand in both of his and warmed it. "What I'm going to try is some good food and a vintage wine. And rather than hover around my doorway all night, why don't you come in and see my place? Would you like a drink before dinner?"

"Love one," she breathed, wishing she had fortified herself before coming over.

He led her into an enormous room filled with so many different things that Jess had to stop and catch her breath before slowly looking around. The walls were white, what there was of them showing. Most of the wall space was taken up with prints, signed and numbered in the corners, and all framed starkly in chrome. None of the pictures looked like they were *of* anything, and at first that made them seem confusing to her. But as she looked at them they seemed pleasing in their shapes and forms and colors, and she felt she could get to like them.

Two long couches covered in velvet were perpendicular to the longest wall, a chrome and glass coffee table between them. The table held only one large crystal ashtray, almost invisible against the glass surface. There was a grand piano in one corner of the room; in another, an antique table used as a bar that held a very large assortment of bottles where Tory was fixing them drinks. She saw a complex stereo system that she now realized was responsible for the background music: something classical that she didn't recognize. In another corner of the room was a comfortable-looking chair and ottoman facing a very large TV set. It seemed to her to be the room of a sophisticated single man, wealthy enough to indulge certain whims, a man who had settled comfortably into his ways. She wondered fleetingly what he would think if he saw how she lived. He would probably feel sorry for her, think her deprived, while in actuality Jess had everything she wanted in her cabin.

The floors were polished wood, bare except for an area rug in an unusual design between the two couches. The room was mostly whites and beiges with all the color coming from the prints on the wall. She was still looking around, noting the details, when Tory handed her a glass of whiskey.

"Well, what do you think?" he asked.

"Very nice. This is the way I always pictured New

101

York millionaires living. It looks like something out of a magazine or a movie."

"A decorator didn't do it, if that's what you're thinking. I put it together myself."

Jess hadn't been thinking that; she had never even known anyone who had used a decorator. She took a sip of her drink. Good whiskey, very smooth. "May I see the rest?"

"Sure. Come on in the kitchen first while I check on the food."

She followed him into a large kitchen from which she had already detected delicious smells. The floor was tile, the counters Butcher Block, and the cabinets appeared to be of a wood-grained metal. Large gleaming appliances were everywhere, and in a corner was a Butcher Block table and four chairs. The table was set for two with placemats, silverware, dishes, and even linen napkins. At least there were no candles or flowers, she thought with amusement. Pots were simmering on the stove, the oven was on, and the sink was already filled with dirty utensils. She saw an electric toaster, a blender, a microwave oven, and several other items she didn't recognize.

"What's this?" she asked, pointing to a small appliance.

"That's an electric ice crusher."

"And this?"

"An electronic coffee grinder."

She gave up asking and just shook her head. She was beginning to feel like Alice in Wonderland. What had happened to the days when people did things for themselves?

"Do you use all these things?" she finally asked.

"Sure, they come in handy."

He led her back through the living room and then down a hall, pausing at the first room they came to. He switched on the light and she stepped inside.

"My favorite room," he said by way of explanation.

It was a study, a workroom with bookshelves lining the walls, a desk covered with manuscripts, and even a typing table with an electric typewriter.

She walked over to get a better look. "If I had electricity, I'd buy one of these," said Jess, looking with envy at the IBM Selectric. "Isn't this one of the ones that even corrects errors?"

He nodded. "How do you manage to get along without electricity?"

"People used to, you know," she said coolly.

"That's because they *had* to."

"It's really no hardship," she assured him. "Anyway my typing improves all the time. Maybe I'd get sloppy if I had a typewriter that did all the work for me."

"Well, maybe you can function in the mountains without electricity, but you sure can't in the city. We've had a couple of blackouts, and it was murder."

She thought of his apartment during a blackout with all the electrical appliances stilled, probably getting a well-deserved rest from all the use he put them to.

She walked over to the desk. Between piles of manuscripts were an electric pencil sharpener, a digital clock, a desk calculator, even an electric stapler. This was indeed a civilized man—and a consumer on a grand scale. "Do you do a lot of work at home?"

"I read manuscripts, do some editing."

"What do you staple?"

"What are you talking about, Jess?"

"This electric stapler. That's what it is, isn't it? What do you use it for?"

"What are you getting at, Jess?"

"I'm just wondering if you actually use all these gadgets or whether you just enjoy buying them."

"What's the difference? I can afford them."

"But do you actually staple anything?" She took a pencil without much point and pushed it into the electric sharpener, amazed at the way it came out sharpened in just seconds. She had an old hand-operated one that always left shavings all over the floor. "Do you really sharpen enough pencils to need this? Or—"

In answer he opened the file drawer of his desk and yanked out one of the files. Inside, neatly stapled, were his canceled checks, arranged according to month.

"You're very neat," observed Jess.

"Yes, I am. Do you have something against neatness too?" He was beginning to sound annoyed.

Jess, who was neat herself, merely shrugged.

Tory put the folder back in the drawer and slammed it shut. "I can't wait to see what you'll say about the bedroom," he muttered.

Don't tell me, thought Jess. A waterbed, a mirrored ceiling, stereo speakers, probably another TV.

He didn't stop to show her the bathroom off the hall but led her straight into his bedroom. Which, she had to admit, was Spartan compared with the rest of the apartment. Done in brown and white, it held only a double bed with a plain beige spread. A long low dresser with a mirror stood against one wall and in a corner was a straight-backed chair. One whole wall was sliding doors; evidently it was a closet.

Jess looked around in silence.

"Well? No questions? No comments?" he asked a little testily.

"I know what everything is," said Jess.

"Perhaps you'd like to inspect the closet," he said, striding over and sliding back the doors.

Jess was stunned into silence at the array of clothes. Two rows of neatly polished shoes ran the length of the room. At least two dozen suits were hung neatly; a special device held an endless amount of ties; and the portion relegated to sport clothes was slight indeed. He stood there waiting for her to comment, but she had nothing to say. All her clothes, winter and summer both, were kept in one metal footlocker, and it still had room to spare.

"What are you trying to prove, Jess? That you're frugal and I'm not? That you save your money and I spend mine? That we have nothing in common, and what the hell are you doing here anyway?"

"I'm not criticizing your life-style, Tory."

"You're doing *exactly* that! And I don't feel like I have to defend it to you either. I'm like most people; I like the good things in life, the luxuries. I work hard for what I have, and I don't think I'd be a better person if I got rid of it all and lived in some empty room and owned one suit of clothes."

"I know that, Tory—"

"You say it, but I don't think you believe it. I think you believe you're above all this, the material comforts of life. Well maybe now it's a lark—twenty-five years old and roughing it in the wilds—but let's see if you're still doing it at thirty. Or forty."

"I'm not going to change, Tory," she said, a look of determination in her eyes.

"Neither am I!"

Jess saw his anger and knew he didn't deserve the way she had been behaving. If she'd gone to visit Allison, she would have admired her furnishings, never behaved as though she thought Alli didn't deserve them. But some perversity in her wouldn't let her treat Tory with the same respect.

"Look, if you'd rather I went home . . ." she murmured.

Tory sighed. "That's right. I slave in a hot kitchen for hours and then you just walk out!" He started to laugh.

"No electric blanket?" she couldn't resist asking as they headed back to the living room.

He gave her a warning look and she subsided. "Just stay in the living room, drink your drink, and dinner will be ready in about five minutes," he said to her.

"Can I help?" she asked, glad that he wasn't still angry with her.

"Since I don't have any animals for you to skin or fish for you to clean, no."

He left her settled down on one of the velvet couches, but as soon as he disappeared into the kitchen she got up and wandered over to the piano. It had been years since she'd been near one, but as a child her parents had insisted she take lessons. Mostly all it had done for her was make her hate the classical music that had taken time from her baseball playing and horseback riding, but still the keys held a kind of lure.

She sat down at the bench and tentatively moved her fingers to the keys. She had once been able to play Chopin rather well, she recalled, but now her fingers couldn't seem to remember how they had once worked. "Chopsticks" didn't present any problem though. Probably because she had played it so often as a child, an event that usually drove her parents to distraction.

She started out slowly, softly at first, but soon was playing what she thought was a rousing rendition of the piece.

"That's better as a duet." Tory was standing behind her, watching her act like a kid with a new toy.

"Prove it," challenged Jess.

He sat down to her right, and as she played the bass part he improvised with all kinds of things, all of them sounding fantastic with "Chopsticks."

"That's pretty good," she said to him.

"A compliment from Jess Haggerty? I don't believe it." He seemed spurred on to greater feats, and soon "Chopsticks" was sounding almost legitimate.

They played for several minutes and then both stopped at the same time.

"What else can you play?" Jess asked him.

"That's my entire repertoire," he declared.

"You have a grand piano so you can play 'Chopsticks'?"

"Are you going to start that again?"

"I think it's kind of great, in a way," she assured him. "A grand piano just for 'Chopsticks'—that's my kind of musician."

"I made up those variations myself," he admitted.

"I was forced to take piano lessons as a kid and all I ever really enjoyed playing was 'Chopsticks,' " said Jess.

"Me too."

"No kidding?"

"No kidding. Used to drive my parents nuts."

"Me too."

"See, Jess. We do have something in common."

"Only *I* don't own a grand piano."

"Why not? They don't require electricity."

"Tory, this piano would take up my entire cabin."

He put an arm around her shoulders. "Wouldn't you like me to take you away from all that?"

"No," she grinned, then added, "Was that a proposal?"

"Just a joke."

"That's what I thought. Just wanted to make sure."

"I wouldn't think of proposing to a man-hating hermit like you. Probably be shot down for even trying."

She laughed. "Probably."

"However—"

"Isn't dinner ready yet? I'm starved."

He took her hand and stood up. "Actually it's probably cold by now. Let's go."

Jess eyed the many small covered dishes on the table as she sat down and spread the napkin across her lap. The odors wafting from them were delicious, albeit strange. If she had to guess what they were going to eat, she'd say Chinese food, because it had that kind of smell. But yet it was somewhat different. Who knows, she thought. *If he took me to an Indian restaurant, this could be anything.*

Tory lifted the tops off the dishes and told her to help herself to everything.

Jess peered into the dishes. "What is it, Tory? Chinese? It kind of smells Chinese, but it doesn't look familiar." She didn't feel like she was complaining; she just liked to know what she was eating.

"It's Szechuan," he answered. "Chinese, but a little different from what you're probably used to."

"I'm not used to any of it. There was a Chinese restaurant in town when I was a kid, but all I ever had was chop suey and rice." And she had eaten that with the greatest reluctance, much preferring when her parents would take her to McDonald's.

"Then this will certainly be different. An education for your palate."

Jess began to put portions of everything on her plate. "What I don't understand, Tory, is why you'd cook it? Couldn't you just send out for it?"

Tory was already eating with gusto. "Of course, but it wouldn't be the same."

"Why not?"

He spread his arms expressively. "It wouldn't be home-cooked."

"What's so great about home-cooked?" Personally Jess had got pretty tired of her own cooking. Being taken out to restaurants in New York was a real treat.

"I told you I'd cook dinner for you."

"Well, I wouldn't have known the difference." She took a portion of meat in her mouth and was just beginning to savor the exquisite taste when something like a red-hot fire started to burn up her throat and threaten her insides. She began to take deep breaths and reached for a glass of water. There wasn't a glass of water, so she grabbed the wineglass and stifled the flames consuming her throat.

"My God, Tory," she gasped. "What's in it?"

Tory was watching her with interest. "It's regular Szechuan—rather highly spiced, but delicious, don't you think?" He was calmly eating his own food and didn't seem to be resorting to wine to wash it down.

Jess felt surprised that she could still speak—and doubtful of taking another bite, hungry as she was. "What's in it, Tory, pure pepper?"

He gave her a condescending look. "The trick, Jess, is to take some rice with every bite. It kind of neutralizes the heat."

Jess looked incredulous at this bit of advice, but tried one of the other dishes, this time taking a portion of rice with it. It was still hot, but not too hot, and the burning sensation in her mouth subsided somewhat.

"The Indian food was pretty hot and you enjoyed it, so I thought you'd like this," he said, apparently enjoying every bite of his.

"I do like it; I'm just not used to swallowing fire. But what's in it that makes it that hot?"

"What difference does it make?"

"Well, I do cook, you know. I might want to try it some time."

"It's pretty difficult, and I doubt you could get all the ingredients where you live," Tory said, obviously not interested in pursuing the subject.

"Like what? What couldn't I get?"

"Oh, different Chinese things. You probably don't have any Chinese living in Wyoming."

"On the contrary, we have quite a few. Chinese restaurants, too."

"Really? In Wyoming?"

"It's not just cowboys and Indians, Tory."

He poured her some more wine. "Tell me, Jess, what do you eat when you're at home?"

"Quit trying to change the subject, Tory. I want to know what you used to cook this?"

"I'll type you up my recipe after dinner, all right?"

"I'd just like you to name one ingredient you used that could make it so hot."

"Well . . . pepper, of course."

"I could figure that out for myself. What *Chinese* ingredient? One of the ones you don't think I can find." She could be just as stubborn as he was.

111

"I don't want to talk about it." He started eating with a vengeance.

"Why are you being so evasive, Tory? I'd think it was some secret family recipe your mother handed down to you, only I don't think you have a Chinese mother."

"Can't we just drop the subject?" For some reason he was beginning to look very uncomfortable.

"What's wrong with talking about food while we're eating dinner?" Jess was like a dog with a bone and wasn't about to let go of the subject until she'd got some satisfaction.

Tory was looking more than uncomfortable now. He was looking plain guilty. "Well, there was something called . . . *nakagawa*."

"*Nakagawa?*"

He nodded.

"That sounds Japanese to me, not Chinese."

"Yeah, it does, doesn't it?"

Jess set down her fork with a clatter. "What's going on here, Tory? I'm not going to eat another bite until you do some explaining."

Tory put down his own fork, took a long drink of his wine, then looked her straight in the eyes. "I sent out for it."

"You *what?*"

"I sent out for it. I got home late, and there wasn't time to cook you anything, so I sent out for it."

"Then why is your kitchen such a mess?"

"I did that so you'd think I cooked it."

Jess looked at him in amazement. "I don't believe this! First you lie about owning jeans, then you lie about cooking dinner. Can I believe anything you say?"

"I don't suppose you'll believe me if I say I generally don't lie."

Jess started to answer with a resounding "No," then instead started to laugh. "*Nakagawa?*" she finally gasped.

He nodded his head. "I knew that was a mistake as soon as I said it, but I couldn't for the life of me think of a Chinese word."

"*Nakagawa!*" She wiped her eyes with her napkin. "How was I to know you knew Japanese from Chinese?"

"It's hard not to know Japanese these days when half the products on the market are made in Japan."

"Yes, but you never buy products."

"That doesn't mean I don't see them. *Nakagawa* sounds like a motorcycle!"

"Listen, I'll cook for you another night," offered Tory.

Jess began eating again. "You don't have to cook for me, Tory. It's a pleasure for me to eat out."

"Yes, but eating out doesn't get you to my apartment."

"You went to all this subterfuge just to get me here and seduce me?"

"You've got it all wrong. I got you here so you could seduce *me*, remember?"

"The way you lie, you've probably got a wife and six children stashed somewhere."

Tory looked affronted. "Do you see any evidence of a woman around here?"

113

"That doesn't prove anything."

"I've never been married, Jess, I swear."

"I know that, Tory, but it's because Allison told me that I believe it, not because you swear. If you'd lie about cooking dinner—"

"Why did Allison tell you?"

There was a long pause while she silently cursed herself for once more speaking before thinking. "I don't remember," she said finally, thinking she was turning into something of a liar herself. Couldn't men and women ever just be honest with each other?

"Did you ask Allison if I was married?"

She looked down at her food. "I might have."

A slow smile was forming on his mouth. "And why were you interested in my marital status?"

"I wasn't the least bit interested in your marital status, Tory. I was only interested in knowing whether it was a married man I was going to the theater with. I don't make it a habit of going out with married men."

"You don't make it a habit of going out with *any* men!"

Jess slammed her napkin on the table and stood up. "Why is it we can't be together ten minutes without fighting?" She waited for an answer and when one wasn't forthcoming, she started to leave the kitchen to get her jacket and go home. Some romantic evening it had turned out to be!

His voice followed her. "I have chocolate cream pie for dessert."

"You're probably lying again," said Jess, paused in the doorway.

"I didn't say I made it. I picked it up at the bakery."

"Chocolate cream pie with Chinese food?"

"Sounds good to me."

It sounded good to Jess too. She went back into the kitchen and took her seat, once more spreading her napkin on her lap. "All right. One piece and then I'm going home."

"When you've tasted my chocolate cream—"

"*Your* chocolate cream pie?"

"My *baker's* chocolate cream pie, you won't want to go home."

He cut her an enormous piece, and it was maybe the best chocolate cream pie she had ever eaten. She could easily have eaten a second helping, but since he didn't offer one she didn't want to open herself up to ridicule. His piece was equally as large, and she couldn't understand why he didn't put on weight. Surely his job was sedentary and she hadn't heard him mention any sports.

"How do you keep in shape?" she asked him.

"I don't climb mountains, if that's what you mean."

"But you don't seem to put on weight."

"We have our ways in New York."

"Like what? I doubt whether you even walk anywhere."

"You're right, I take a taxi to my health club."

"Health club? What do you do there?"

"Work out on the Nautilus equipment."

"What do you need equipment for? You could exercise right here at home."

115

"Jess, if you're going to start another argument, I'm just going to have to shut you up."

Jess frowned. "I thought we were having a conversation."

"That didn't sound like a conversation to me. It sounded like you were criticizing my life-style again and asking for an argument."

Jess considered this for a moment and found some merit in what he said. "I think you're right. I guess I like to argue, or else I'm just not used to talking to people."

"I like to argue, too, but not all the time." She smiled at him. "What else do you have in mind?"

He stood up and held out his hand to her. "Come see my terrace. The romantic view might get you in the mood."

Actually, although she would have hated to admit it to anyone, the arguing with him was getting her in the mood. As she recalled, she and Mark had spent half their time arguing and then making up, and she had enjoyed every minute of it. Robert had been more disposed to lecture than to argue, Jess remembered. She felt stimulated by once more arguing with a man. And Tory seemed very adept at it; he even got the better of her occasionally.

A door from the kitchen led out to a terrace about four feet by fifteen. She walked over to the railing and leaned over, looking down. Below she could see an occasional car passing by.

Tory grabbed her around the waist and pulled her back. "Better not lean on that."

116

"Why not, isn't it safe?"

"Yes, it's sturdy enough, but some people get dizzy from heights."

Jess remembered climbing the steep sides of mountains and never getting dizzy, only exhilarated, but didn't say anything.

"Look over there," he was saying. "Isn't that a great view?"

"Is that the Empire State Building lit up in colors?"

"Yes. It's still my favorite."

She started to shiver from the cold. "It's beautiful. From my hotel room I can see the park."

He put his arm around her and drew her close to him. "That's a romantic view too."

"It's really nothing compared to the view of the mountains I have at home," said Jess complacently.

He dropped his arm. "Are we going to argue views now?"

She laughed. "If you want to."

"That's not what I had in mind." He pulled her around to face him and leaned down to cover her mouth with his. It would have been decidedly romantic if it had been warmer out, but as it was she felt like she was freezing to death. The air felt damp as though it might rain.

He stopped kissing her and looked down into her eyes. "What are you thinking about, Jess?" he asked in a soft voice.

"I'm thinking how cold it is out here," she said, rubbing her arms with her hands.

He sighed. "So much for romantic terraces. Come on inside and I'll fix us some brandy."

Once in the living room he changed the cassette on the stereo and dimmed the lights. He poured them each a snifter of brandy, then settled them side by side on one of the couches. As the music began—a singer singing in French—he put his arm around her and drew her head down on his shoulder.

"This is nice, isn't it?" he murmured. "Just sitting here peacefully, listening to romantic music. I'd light some candles, but I don't remember where I put them."

"What's romantic about the music?" she asked him.

"I find French romantic, don't you?"

"Sometimes, but this is a political song," she pointed out.

He chuckled. "It couldn't be. Listen to that sad refrain. It's probably about lost love, or unrequited love or something. The French are famous for that."

"Tory, don't you understand French?"

He shook his head. "I had German in school."

"Well, I had French, and what he's singing about isn't romantic. It's about the oppressed masses."

"I never knew that. I always thought it sounded romantic."

"Do you want me to translate it for you?"

He turned to her. "No, Jess, that's the last thing I want." He moved her head so that it was facing him, then effectively cut off any further remarks by once again closing his mouth over hers.

With a satisfied sigh Jess moved sideways on the

couch and put her arms around his neck, then closed her eyes and gave herself over to his kiss. His tongue parted her lips and her mouth opened to allow it entrance, and then their tongues were dueling with the same intensity with which they argued, but Jess found this even more stimulating.

He pushed her back along the couch until her head was resting on the arm, then moved his body so that it was half beside her and half on top of her. She turned to him, pressing her body along the length of his, almost willing them to be joined. She was feeling the whiskey, the wine, the brandy. She was also feeling much, much more. She was remembering all the times she had made love, and wanting it again. Wanting it with this one man in particular, a man who stirred her mind as well as her body.

His hand went to the buttons on her shirt and slowly began to undo them until first one and then the other breast fell free from its folds, and then his hand was doing lovely things to them, causing them to slowly rise and then to peak. She arched her body against his hand, wishing he'd remove all of her re-straining clothes. Her jeans were tight—uncomfort-able after the big meal she had eaten—and she longed to be free of them, and for him to be free of his so that they could lie together and explore each other's bodies.

She moaned and moved even closer to him. His lips left hers and began to travel downward. He kissed the hollows of her throat, then moved down farther, circling her breasts, tasting them with his tongue, and then moving in on one to suck her nipple

119

and make her cry out with the pleasure of it. His other hand moved to the belt on her jeans, finally getting it undone, and then trying to unzip her pants. She sucked in her stomach, trying to make them looser and easier to undo, finally reaching down herself and tugging down the zipper. She lifted her body so that he could remove them, but he got them as far as her boots and then they stuck and would go no farther. With a sigh Jess sat up on the couch. Why didn't it ever happen the way it did in books, where clothes just somehow miraculously came off without any problems? She tugged on first one boot and then the other, took off her socks, then stood up and stepped out of her jeans. Her shirt was hanging open down the front, and she also let that fall to the floor, then stood there in just her cotton panties.

He reached out his arms to her, but she shook her head. "You too. You get undressed, Tory."

He began to remove his clothes, his eyes watching her all the while, gleaming with desire as she stepped out of her panties and stood there naked, waiting for him.

Instead of pulling her back on the couch, he took her hand and led her down the hall to his bedroom, leaving just the hall light on for illumination.

Once on the bed he kissed her again, long kisses that held out promise of what was to come. She moved her hands over his body as they kissed, loving the feel of his chest hair scratching against her breasts. He was firm and hard all over, as fit as she was, and she loved the feel of his body. He moved once again to her breasts and sucked on the nipples

120

lovingly, longingly, one by one, as she felt herself losing all semblance of control. He was kissing her stomach now, and then the warm place between her legs, and she was thrashing around on the bed, saying his name, wanting him to do more, more. . . .

When he gently parted her legs, she was ready and expectant, eager and yet a little frightened that the lovemaking might not live up to her expectations. She didn't want to be disappointed in him. She just couldn't be disappointed in him. She cared too much. Far too much.

And then all uncertainty vanished as they merged and became one. She thrust up at him, crying out, keeping her eyes open and watching his face, gripping his shoulders, her fingers digging into his skin, and then it was total soaring pleasure as the rhythm increased and the intensity of her feelings overwhelmed her. They were both trying to hold back, to keep on the sensitive edge for a few more moments, but they couldn't, and then she was crying with relief and pleasure and kissing his face, her back arching convulsively until the moment was over and they held on to each other, and he was whispering endearments in her ear, words she barely heard in the shattering state he had brought her to.

He finally moved off her and onto his side, resting on one elbow and looking down at her. "Are you feeling as good as I am?" he finally asked her, his voice strangely hoarse.

At first Jess couldn't find a voice in which to an-

121

swer. Then she found a voice that didn't sound anything like her own and said, "Better. Even better."

He lifted a mocking brow. "Are we now going to argue about which of us feels better?"

"Well, I'm sure it's been a lot longer for me. I had forgotten how much I liked it."

"I won't dispute that you're the celibate in the group," he quipped. "Former celibate anyway."

"I've lost my standing," said Jess.

"Yes, you have. Aren't you glad?"

She paused to consider his question for a moment, teasing him, and then she said, "Yes, I am. Glad."

He leaned back on the pillow beside her. "What now, Jess?"

"What do you mean, what now?"

"Where do we go from here?"

She reached for him, but he took her hands and held them. "I'm not talking about sex; I'm talking about us."

"Do we have to talk now, Tory?"

He looked down at himself, as though surprised to find he was ready again, and then chuckled. "No, I guess we don't have to talk about it now."

Their second joining was an exploration of possibilities. They made love slowly, barely moving, lingering over surfaces and textures, savoring the short gasps that passed for breathing, holding back until it was no longer feasible and the fault opened and, clinging to each other, they fell in. And this time Jess heard herself crying out, but it was more than his name she was calling. "I love you, Tory, I love you," she was saying, and he was answering, "Yes, of course you do, I love you too," and it seemed right at the moment, right and true, and they held each other tightly, as though afraid to let go.

Later, when they were sitting in his kitchen having coffee, she apologized for getting carried away.

"No need to apologize," he assured her, "you were marvelous."

She could feel herself blushing. "I'm not talking about the sex. I meant the things I said. . . ."

He eyed her complacently across the table. "I always thought it was a romantic notion, hopelessly false, but I was wrong. There is such a thing as love at first sight, and I think we fell into it, Jess. Don't deny it; you feel the same way I do."

"Tory, I think you're confusing love with lust."

His eyes moved slowly down her still-naked body. "If it was just lust, Jess, anyone would do. It's you I want."

Jess lowered her eyes. "Well, what's the point of love? We live twenty-five hundred miles apart."

"That can be overcome."

She looked at him. "You planning on moving to Wyoming?"

"You know I can't do that."

"Well, I couldn't live in a city," Jess said forcefully, then drank the last of her coffee and stood up. "And I think it's time I go home. I start work in the morning, remember?"

They both began to retrieve their clothes from the living room floor and get dressed. "Why don't you stay here, Jess? You can just use the hotel room for when you're coaching Philip."

Tory's bed might have been just fine for making love, but she didn't want to sleep in it. Too soft by far. "I prefer the hotel."

"Come on, the Plaza's no more Spartan than my apartment. And if all the electrical appliances bother you so much, I'll unplug them."

She shook her head slowly. "I don't want to get used to something I might miss when I have to leave."

"You don't have to leave, you know."

She buckled her belt and went to the hall closet for her jacket. "I do eventually."

He got a jacket of his own out and put it on. "I don't want to argue with you any more tonight; we'll discuss it later. Come on, I'll find a taxi and take you home."

"You don't need to go with me."

"No more arguments, Jess!"

It was hard leaving him when they got to the hotel. She clung to him in the taxi, returning his kisses and wishing she hadn't been so stubborn about going home. It would have been nice to wake up with him in the morning; nice for them to have breakfast together.

"How about tonight?" he asked her as she got out of the cab.

She smiled down at him. "Are you going to cook dinner for me again?"

He laughed. "I thought I'd let Manny's wife do that. They've invited us to dinner if you want to go. I told him I'd have to ask you first."

124

"It's fine with me," she told him, although she would have preferred being alone with him at night.

"Good. We'll pick you up after work then, and Manny will drive us out."

"Out where?"

"They live on the Island."

"What island?"

"Long Island. I think you'll like it."

An island? thought Jess, walking into the hotel. This should be interesting.

CHAPTER EIGHT

Tory rode in the front seat with Manny and Jess, and Allison—who had also been invited to dinner—sat in back. The traffic was bumper-to-bumper going out of the city, and Jess could begin to realize just why Manny was such a nervous person. If she had to drive in traffic like this twice a day, she'd be nervous too.

"Is the traffic always this bad?" Jess finally asked Manny, who was cursing under his breath at the long stream of cars in front of them and lighting what must have been his dozenth cigarette since they had started out.

"It's worse on Mondays and Fridays," he answered.

"How do you stand it?" asked Jess, feeling very much like getting out of the car and walking, a mode of transportation that would have been faster at that moment.

He looked at her in the rearview mirror. "Listen, it's worth it to live out of the city. At least you can breathe clean air on the Island."

Jess rolled down the window a little to let out some

of the smoke. "Why not move the business to the island?" Jess suggested.

"Yeah, Tory, why don't we?" asked Manny.

"So *I* can commute instead of *you?*"

"You'd love living out there," Manny enthused. "Lots of space, relatively little crime—"

"Forget it, Manny," Tory broke in. "Businesses belong in the city."

"So do actresses," muttered Allison, then turned to Jess. "How did it go today?"

"Just great," said Jess. "Phil is intelligent and funny and nice—it was a pleasure working with him."

"What did you actually do?"

"I gave him copies of all my books to read, and he said he'd start on them tonight. Mostly we just walked around Central Park and talked. He's tireless too; I must have walked him miles, but he never complained."

"We're paying the guy to walk around the park with her all day?" groaned Manny.

"The hotel room was too claustrophobic," said Jess.

"A *suite* at the *Plaza* gives you claustrophobia?" Manny looked over his shoulder at her with disbelief in his eyes.

"The suite is fine. More room than I need actually. I just find being indoors all day too confining. Anyway we can talk just as well in the park as we can in the hotel. We talked about writing in general and I told him about the Old West, what I know of it. Tomorrow we're going to find some clothes for him."

127

"A cowboy outfit?" asked Allison.

"Maybe a hat and some boots," said Jess, "if they have such things in the city. He's got his own jeans and shirts."

"Why don't you get him a *real* cowboy outfit?" asked Manny. "You know, like Roy Rogers or something."

"Because only Roy Rogers dresses like that," Jess informed him. "I want him to dress like me."

Manny's eyes in the rearview mirror gave her the once-over. "Yeah, I guess he could get away with that. By the way, Jess, you'll like my wife—she's a writer too."

"What does she write?" asked Jess, thinking maybe she'd read something by her.

"Cookbooks. She writes under her maiden name, Betty Barker."

Jess had never read a cookbook in her life. "Has your wife written any cookbooks on Szechuan cooking?" she asked Manny in a deceptively innocent voice.

Tory turned around and gave her a threatening look, which she ignored.

"I don't think so, Jess. Why?"

"Knock it off, Jess," warned Tory.

"By the way," asked Allison, "what did Tory cook for you last night?"

"You cooked for her?" asked Manny.

Tory seemed intent on the traffic ahead and didn't answer.

"It was Szechuan," Jess told Allison.

"Really? Was it good?"

"Delicious, once I got the hang of eating it without burning up."

"I know what you mean," said Allison.

Manny turned to Tory. "You cook Szechuan? Maybe you could give my wife your recipes. I really love Szechuan."

"I don't have any recipes," said Tory in a final tone.

"I doubt whether your wife could find all the ingredients, Manny," said Jess. "There's stuff like . . . like *nakagawa* that would probably be hard to find."

Tory made a choking noise in the front seat, and Jess decided to let him off the hook.

They got to the Midtown Tunnel, and once through, the traffic lightened somewhat.

It was another good hour's drive after that, and while Tory and Manny discussed business in the front seat, Allison told Jess stories about funny things that had happened to her at auditions.

"I was in a play just once," Jess confided. "Our sixth-grade graduation play. And when I got on stage, I completely froze and forgot all my lines. I think it might have been the worst experience of my life."

"I guess it's a good thing we hired an actor to play you, then," said Allison.

Jess kept waiting for them to cross a huge body of water and was surprised when Manny finally turned into a circular driveway and stopped in front of a white Colonial house that was all lighted up. "We're here, folks," he announced.

"This is an island?" asked Jess.

"Sure, Long Island," Manny told her.

"Where's the water?"

"A few miles away."

Tory got out and opened the rear door for them, then said to Jess: "How do you like it? Manny's got half an acre; lots of trees and lawn. Real country living, isn't it?"

Jess looked at the row of houses across the street, the houses flanking Manny's and all the cars in the street. "Where I come from, this is called city living," she told him.

"How can you say that?" asked Tory. "Look, no skyscrapers, no subways, no crowds of people—you can even see the stars!"

"I don't think it's going to work, Tory," said Manny.

"What's not going to work?" asked Jess.

"Tory figured if you saw Long Island, it would seem like home to you. He says you don't like the city."

"I doubt this compares with the Rockies," said Allison, leading the way to the front door. "Why can't you just accept that she likes where she lives, Tory? You can't convert everyone to New York, you know."

Jess looked over at Tory and winked. "Good try," she told him softly.

As the others walked to the door ahead of them, he put his arm around her and gave her a quick hug. "Maybe if you saw it in daylight, you'd change your mind."

"I doubt it," she said, and then the door was opened by a plump freckle-faced woman wearing an honest-to-God apron over polyester pants and a flowered blouse.

"I'm Betty," she said, holding out her hand to Jess. "And I'm real pleased you could come to dinner. I didn't know what a cowgirl would like, so I just fixed prime ribs," she apologized.

"That's my favorite," Jess assured her, then was ushered into a living room cluttered with children's toys, ruffled lamps, and needlepoint cushions on every available piece of furniture. Family photographs were lined up on the mantel; a white cat was asleep in a rocking chair; a bag of knitting was on the floor beside it.

The men excused themselves, and Betty sat down with them in the living room. "We girls can get acquainted," she said to them. "Dinner won't be ready for another half hour yet."

She told them about her two young children—both, to Jess's relief, already upstairs in bed—then regaled Jess and Allison with stories of her cooking disasters, the children's exploits, and suburban living in general. Allison seemed to be coping; Jess was doing her best to pay attention, but it was a losing battle. Betty was a nonstop talker—and a bore to the bargain. Jess finally excused herself to go to the bathroom, Betty pointing the way to it down the hall.

On the way there she passed a room, looked in, and saw Manny and Tory playing a game of pool.

"Are we allowed in the game?" Jess asked them. Manny looked up from a shot he was making.

131

"Betty calls this my playroom," he said. "She never comes in here except to clean, and it's off limits to the kids."

Jess glanced around and saw a poker table set up in one corner and a bar in another. This was her kind of room. She noticed the two men had drinks, so she walked over to the bar and poured herself some whiskey. She watched as Manny made the shot and missed, leaving Tory in good position.

"You play pool, Jess?" asked Tory.

"A little."

"I'll play you a game as soon as I've beaten Manny, which shouldn't take much longer."

"You ought to have Betty show you the kitchen," Manny suggested to her. "It's really something— looks like it belongs to a professional cook."

Jess was taking the darts out of a board that hung on the wall. "Does she have lots of electrical gadgets?"

"Oh, hell, yes—she has everything," Manny told her.

"Then Tory would probably be more interested," said Jess, throwing the darts and hitting four bull's-eyes in a row.

"If you're trying to make me miss my shot, you're not going to succeed," said Tory, sinking one of the balls in a corner pocket.

"Watch out, Tory, she's probably trying to hustle you at pool. She's a real demon at the dart board," said Manny.

"Nobody hustles me at pool."

Jess wandered over to the poker table and sat

down. "Can we play cards after dinner?" she asked Manny.

He shrugged. "I guess so, if Allison knows how to play."

"If Allison knows how to play what?" asked Allison from the doorway.

"Poker," said Jess.

Allison walked over and joined her at the table. "Thanks for deserting me," she said to Jess under her breath.

"You looked like you were doing just fine."

Allison shook her head at the memory, then turned to Manny. "Sure, I can play poker. What do you think actors do backstage?"

"It'll be for money," warned Tory. "Some people, being misers, maybe won't like playing for money."

Jess laughed. "That would only bother me if I lost," she told him. "I don't plan on losing."

"I think that was a challenge, Tory," said Manny, watching in frustration as Tory cleaned the table of balls.

"You're on, Jess," Tory said to her. "You want to break?"

Jess nodded as she got up. She took the cue stick from Manny, chalked the end, then positioned the ball to make the break. She put a spin on the ball that sent it flying, sinking two balls and leaving her in perfect position for a third.

Manny was congratulating her when Betty came to the door and announced that dinner was ready.

Jess looked over at Tory. "Saved by dinner."

"We'll continue it afterward," he promised her, a look of challenge in his dark eyes.

The dinner was delicious, the conversation less than stimulating, and after Betty's initial surprise that they were going to play poker after dinner, she said, "Well, that will be a treat! I don't often get to play with the boys."

Betty declined Jess's offer to help clean up, and she and Tory resumed the game of pool. It was pretty even all the way, and when she finally did beat him, it was mostly because it was her turn at the right time. After that, Betty joined them, and they set up for a game of poker.

They played dealer's choice, which was fine with Jess except that whenever it was Betty's turn, they played so many strange games with so many wild cards, Jess always ended up losing that hand. In a serious game she would have dropped out, but not wanting to be impolite, she stayed in.

When Allison finally noticed it was one in the morning, the game broke up. Jess hadn't lost, but she hadn't won much either. Allison, surprisingly enough, turned out to be the big winner and didn't let them forget it for a moment.

"It's too late for you to go back to the city," Betty said to them. "Why don't you stay over? We've got plenty of room."

"Sure. We can all drive in together in the morning," said Manny.

"It's all right with me," said Allison.

Tory looked at Jess for her opinion. "Won't they think it strange at the hotel if I don't show up?"

"Honey," said Manny, "they don't care *what* you do as long as the room is paid for."

"Well, let's see," said Betty. "There's an extra bed in Cindy's room that Alli can use, and the couch in the living room opens into a bed . . . and . . ." she looked at Manny for further advice.

"I can sleep on the pool table," joked Tory.

Jess looked at Betty. "Tory can have the couch. I always sleep on the floor, so I can sleep anywhere. Just give me a couple of blankets, and I'll be fine."

"No need to be a martyr, Jess," said Manny.

"I'll sleep on the floor," said Tory.

"Look, I'm serious," Jess assured them. "I'm sleeping on the floor at the hotel, there's no reason why I can't here."

"There were *two* beds in that room as I recall," said Allison.

"Yes, but I don't use them. I don't like those beds—they're too soft."

Betty started to protest again, but Tory interrupted her. "If she likes sleeping on the floor, let her sleep on the floor. Probably better for the back anyway."

Jess also started to turn down Betty's later offer of a nightgown, then realized that with so many people in the house she couldn't very well sleep nude. She did, however, feel extremely silly in the pink nylon-and-lace creation she was given to wear. Since Tory was sleeping in the living room, Jess opted for Manny's "playroom" and curled up comfortably at one end of the pool table. She was tired, not used to staying up so late two nights in a row, and was just

135

about asleep when she heard someone coming stealthily into the room.

There was a sharp sound, a low curse, and then the light went on, and Jess saw Tory, clad in pajamas several sizes too large for him.

"What are you doing in here?" she hissed at him.

He held up his hands in surrender. "Nothing immoral. I just wanted to talk to you."

"Talk to me in the morning!"

"This is private," he said, turning off the light and finding his way to her side in the dark. "Incidentally you look quite fetching in that pink thing."

"Yeah, and you look pretty good in Manny's pajamas."

He got down beside her on the floor and took her in his arms.

"I thought you said you wanted to talk."

"Well, it probably won't do any good, but I was going to ask you if you'd consider suburban living."

"No, it won't do any good. And whom was I to consider it with—*you?*"

"That was the idea."

"Is this a proposal, Tory?"

"Not necessarily. Maybe I just want to live with you."

"Well, the answer is no. If I wanted to live in a place like this, I'd move to Rocky Springs."

"We could get more acreage than this. I really think you'd like some parts of the Island. There's woods and everything."

"Are there deer?"

"I don't think so."

"Bears? Foxes?"

"I sincerely hope not."

"Streams, waterfalls?"

"No, and no mountains either."

"No, thanks, Tory."

"If we love each other, we ought to find a way to be together. Listen, I'm not crazy about Long Island either. I like the city. But I'd be willing to move here if it would make you happy."

"Look, Tory, it's not only Long Island I don't like. I don't like to cook, I can't knit, I have no interest in learning needlepoint, and I most emphatically don't want two children and a station wagon. If you want a wife, Tory, or even a live-in lady, I'm really not the right person for you."

His hand moved beneath her nightgown and started to caress her breast. "I just want you, Jess," he murmured, leaning over her and kissing her lovingly.

Jess moved aside the blanket and rolled toward him, one hand unbuttoning his pajama top so that she could feel his naked chest. "We shouldn't be doing this, Tory," she mumbled beneath the kiss.

"I know, but I want you so badly. Anyway everyone else is upstairs. Just don't scream out in passion."

"I *never* scream out," she protested, but then his mouth was covering hers, and she gave herself up to his kisses and caresses.

He slipped off his pajama bottoms and rolled her on top of him, then instructed her in some variations of what they had done the previous night. Jess was a quick, avid learner, and the last coherent thought she had before succumbing completely to her passion was that soft beds really weren't good for anything at all; the floor was a whole lot better!

CHAPTER NINE

Tory called her Friday morning just as she and Philip were getting ready to leave the suite and asked her if she'd spend the weekend with him at his place.

Jess, who thought that was a marvelous idea, instantly agreed.

"You didn't even give me a chance to use all the arguments I had," complained Tory.

"We could start over and I'll say no."

"No, never mind, I might lose the argument," said Tory, a hint of laughter in his voice.

"Anyway I'd like one weekend to remember you by," Jess told him.

There was a silence on the phone. "There's no way you're going to forget me, Jess—I'm not going to let you."

Jess glanced at Philip, who was leaning against the door. "I can't talk now, Tory—Philip is here."

"You're the teacher. Send him out of the room."

"I'll see you tonight, Tory. About eight?"

"Eight's fine, love. Take care of yourself."

"You too, Tory."

She didn't at all mind the idea of a weekend with

Tory. It would be nice to spend entire nights in his arms, and his apartment did have certain advantages over her hotel suite. They could cook there, and have long, lazy breakfasts in bed. Play duets on the piano, maybe spend long, lazy afternoons in bed. And evenings. . . .

"Got a romance going with the boss?" Phil kidded her.

Jess gave him a wry smile. "I'm afraid so, and it wasn't a very good idea."

"Why not? He seemed like a nice guy."

"There's a little problem of living twenty-five hundred miles apart."

"Why not move to New York?"

"I don't even like small cities, Phil."

"The thing to do in New York is get to know it by neighborhoods. Each neighborhood is like a small town. Have you seen Greenwich Village yet?"

She shook her head.

"You might like it better down there. It's not quite so overwhelming."

"I like the mountains."

"I know you do, Jess, but I don't see how you can expect him to move to your cabin. It sounds great for a writer, but what would *he* do there?"

"Tell me something, Phil. Why do men always insist on having everything their way?"

Phil smiled. "I don't think it's just men, Jess. Everyone wants everything his way—or her way—and the strongest wins out, that's all."

"Exactly! Well, I've gotten pretty strong," she said

in a tone of voice that effectively terminated that particular conversation.

They were going to spend the morning looking for boots and a hat for Phil. They hadn't done it the previous day because Phil had been so enthused about Jess's books, they had spent the whole day discussing them. Now Phil told her that he was pretty sure they could find boots in one of the shoe stores along 34th Street, but he had no idea where a cowboy hat could be purchased in the city.

They walked south on Broadway, the bright sun offsetting the cool breeze that was coming in over the river. The neighborhood quickly began to deteriorate as they hit the Forties, and soon Jess was looking in dismay at bag ladies huddled in doorways and an occasional drunk passed out on the sidewalk. The sidewalks were crowded, and Phil took her arm so that they wouldn't get separated.

Near 42nd Street, as they were passing movie houses showing films whose titles Jess didn't even care to read, she spotted a beautifully dressed young man and pointed him out to Phil.

"Look, he's wearing just the kind of hat you should have. Do you want me to ask him where he bought it?"

Phil took one look in the man's direction and shook his head. "I don't think that would be a very good idea, Jess."

"Why not? He might have purchased it around here."

"Forget it, Jess."

"But *why?*"

"Let's just say he's probably got a string of girls working this area right now. I doubt he'd want to be disturbed."

Jess took another quick look at the man in question, then shut up about it.

When they got to 34th Street, Phil insisted on taking her on a tour of Macy's, the largest department store in the world, or so he said. She was appalled by the number of shoppers who seemed in such a hurry to part with their money. No wonder Tory was such a consumer, she thought, living in a city that seemed exclusively designed for consumers. Not only did the stores have everything imaginable to buy, but the sidewalks outside the stores were filled with vendors selling some of the same items, only cheaper. Jess and Phil could hardly take a step, inside or outside the stores, without someone trying to sell them something.

Phil found a pair of boots that were comfortable and looked right for the part, then had the brilliant idea that they could perhaps rent him a cowboy hat at one of the theatrical supply places in the city. He explained to Jess that they rented items for use in plays, and they'd probably have everything.

They took a subway, another revelation to Jess, down to 14th Street, and sure enough, they were able to rent him a Stetson, which, when on his head, seemed to change his whole appearance. Jess wanted him to wear it, but Phil was reluctant to walk around the city looking like a cowboy.

They walked from 14th Street to Greenwich Village, and Jess found she did like it. The buildings were lower, the streets lined with trees, and the section where they had lunch was filled with college students; it reminded her of the college town where she had attended school.

But the pretty park they walked through after lunch was filled with drug peddlers; the sidewalks were so crowded they often had to step off the curbs; and it seemed to Jess that just trying to cross a street was taking your life into your hands. If this was the best New York had to offer, she wanted no part of it.

Since Phil lived in the Village, and they had accomplished what they had set out to do, she let him out of class early and headed uptown by herself. Along Fifth Avenue she stopped to browse in a couple of bookstores and was delighted when she saw they carried copies of her books. She had never before actually seen them in a store, and she stood around the section marked WESTERNS hoping someone would come along and buy one. No one did, however, so she moved on to where mysteries were sold, and bought a few she hadn't been able to find at home. Much as she disliked New York, she had to admit it had two things better than Wyoming— better restaurants and better bookstores. She consoled herself with the thought that, were she to stay in the city, she'd probably spend far too much money in both.

Jess arrived at Tory's at eight, hoping they were going to spend a quiet evening at home.

No such luck. Tory met her at the door, relieved her of her backpack, which he set down in the entry hall, then hurried her out the door. "I got us two tickets to *Coppélia*," he explained as they waited for the elevator.

"What's that?"

"A ballet."

She turned to him with a look of mischief in her eyes. "You *really* like ballet? I thought you were kidding about that."

Tory looked surprised. "I wouldn't kid about ballet. You like it, don't you?"

"I don't know; I've never seen one." She thought she remembered watching *The Nutcracker Suite* once on television when she was a child, but couldn't recall much about it.

They took a taxi to Lincoln Center, where Tory didn't even give her time to look at the Chagall murals, but just hustled her inside the theater and to their orchestra seats. The lights were already dimming, and then the music began.

The set was elaborate, the costumes colorful, the dancers graceful, and the music soothing. Nevertheless, fifteen minutes into the ballet Jess found herself yawning and wondering what it was Tory liked about ballet. *She* certainly wasn't interested in some nonsensical story about a wooden doll. It wasn't even as interesting as Pinocchio.

Tory, however, seemed thoroughly engrossed, so she tried to think about other things and managed to stay awake until the first intermission.

"Would you like a drink?" Tory asked her.

"I'd like more than a drink," Jess told him, hoping

144

what she was about to say wouldn't precipitate another fight.

"I believe that's all they have."

"I'd like dinner, several drinks, and I'd very much like not to have to see the rest of that ballet."

His forehead furrowed. "You didn't like it?"

"I think the problem is, Tory, that I'm not a good spectator. I prefer doing things to watching other people do them. I even have trouble sitting still for an entire movie, and I hate television."

"But can't you appreciate the talent, the craft involved?"

"I'd rather appreciate it in retrospect over a good dinner. Unless you want to stay and see how it ends."

"I *know* how it ends; this isn't the first time I've seen it."

Jess's eyes widened. "And you'd sit through it *again?*"

"It's like opera, Jess. You see the same one over and over to compare performances."

"I don't even read *books* twice," Jess said, thinking it a waste of time when there were always new ones waiting to be read.

Tory stood up and helped her on with her jacket. "It's you I'm trying to entertain, so if you don't want to stay, that's okay with me. I can always go to the ballet."

Once out of the theater he took her hand and headed for the nearest corner. "There's an Italian restaurant right across the street that's pretty good. I was going to take you to Little Italy, but you might starve to death on the way downtown."

Jess wouldn't argue with that. She hadn't had a bite to eat since lunch, and that had only been a hamburger and fries with Phil.

The restaurant was in green and white with red-and-white checked tablecloths and candles on each table. She ordered veal parmigiana with a side order of spaghetti, and started right in on the bread basket on the table.

Tory poured them each some red wine, then lifted his glass in a toast. "To us," he said, his eyes warm as he gazed at her.

Jess took a sip of her wine. "Tell me something, Tory."

"Anything."

"What you said about love at first sight. Was that really true?"

"Absolutely. I knew right away you were for me."

"But why? What was it about me? I really find it hard to believe my looks just struck you dead."

"I liked the way you looked, but it wasn't that. It was the way you held yourself, your attitude. You seemed so self-possessed, so free of all restraints."

"You mean, I seemed independent."

"I guess so. Of course I had no idea *how* independent."

Jess slowly buttered a breadstick. "And now you want to change that."

"I don't want you dependent, Jess. I wouldn't cage you in."

"I feel caged in in New York."

"I know, and I guess I don't understand that. I've always thought New York held the opportunity to

146

do or be whatever you wanted." He paused for a moment, and then asked, "What about you, Jess? What did you think of me when we met?"

"You really want to know the truth?"

"Apart from being disappointed I wasn't a distinguished gentleman."

"I didn't even think about that. The truth is, Tory, *your* looks almost did strike me dead. You look exactly like I always pictured Boots Ryan looking."

"No kidding?" He didn't sound pleased.

"Except for the clothes, of course, and the fact that Boots is rangier. Other than that, you're the spitting image of my hero."

"So you weren't attracted to *me.* You were attracted to some character you made up, and I just happened to look like him."

Jess couldn't understand what he was getting upset about. "What's the matter with that?"

"I'd rather you were attracted to *me.*"

"I *am* attracted to you. But you also look just like Boots."

"Do I act like Boots?"

"Not at all! Boots is honest, for one thing, and not so argumentative."

Tory's eyes narrowed as he poured himself some more wine. He started to speak, then instead took a drink.

"Look, Tory, you should take it as a compliment. Boots was my ideal in a man, which really means that you are."

"No kidding?"

"Yes. He's everything I think a man should be."

147

"He's not much of a talker though, is he?"

"Well, no. But usually I don't like men who talk a lot."

"And he's a loner, if I'm not mistaken."

"Tory, he has some of my characteristics too. That's only natural when I'm writing the books."

"When we were making love, were you thinking of me as Boots?"

"That's a really stupid question, Tory. I don't ever imagine making love to fictional characters."

Tory didn't say anything to that, and then the food arrived and Jess concentrated on eating, sorry that they were arguing again. She had wanted the weekend to be perfect, something she could think about when she was back in Wyoming, but so far all she had done was spoil the ballet for him and then insult him by comparing him to Boots.

"Are you angry with me now?" she finally asked him.

He gave her a smile that didn't quite reach his eyes. "No, not at all. It's just a strange idea to get used to. What would you like to do tonight? Anything special you'd like to see in the city?"

"What I'd really like to do is go home and relax. I've been out every night since I got here."

Tory gave her a wicked smile. "Sounds good to me."

"And," she continued, "I'd like to walk home. I'm eating far too much with too little exercise."

He reached across the table and took her hand. "We can exercise when we get home."

"It's not that far, Tory; we can walk it easily." She

148

removed her hand, suddenly wanting to do far more than just hold hands with him.

"Jess, we're in the West Sixties and I live in the East Thirties. That's quite a walk."

"If I can manage it, you should be able to. What good is that health club of yours if you can't even walk?"

"Whatever you say," he told her, paying the check and leading her out the door. The night air was cold, which Jess found invigorating, and they started out toward 59th Street.

Walking along the south side of the park, Tory stopped for a moment and pulled her to him. He kissed her on the lips for a long, luxurious moment, unmindful of the pedestrians walking past. "Don't you wish we were home right now?" he murmured, pulling her body tightly against his.

"Umm, yes," agreed Jess, moving her hands up under his jacket and feeling the muscles in his back.

He stopped kissing her. "If we had taken a taxi, we would be!"

Jess stepped back from him. "We have all night, Tory, what's the hurry?"

"It'll take all night to walk home!"

"Are you tired already?" she asked, taunting him. "We've only been walking a few minutes."

"No, I'm not tired," he said, taking her hand and resuming the pace. "I just want you, that's all, and it's a little too public out here."

Jess squeezed his hand. "We could always go in the park. I've found some very secluded spots in there."

"The muggers have probably found the same spots."

"Then I guess you'll just have to wait, won't you?"

Tory walked the rest of the distance home at a very fast pace and in complete silence. Jess found both refreshing. She was eager to get home with Tory too, but she was enjoying the anticipation, and they had the whole weekend ahead of them.

When they finally reached the elevator of his building, he turned to her and unbuttoned her jacket, then reached inside to cup her breasts with his cold hands. She shivered, but not just from the cold, and leaned against him. Then he began kissing her, his hands making patterns of circles around her hard nipples, and she felt herself begin to disintegrate into isolated sensations, fired by the passion that had been steadily building in her on the long walk home.

Her shirt was half open by the time the elevator reached his floor, and they practically ran down the hall to his apartment, Tory pushing her inside the door as soon as he had opened it.

He turned on the light in the entry hall, then pulled her jacket off her shoulders, letting it fall to the floor. As his fingers undid the rest of the buttons on her shirt, she opened his jacket, then his shirt, then pressed her bare breasts against his furry chest as they each fumbled with their pants, getting them down and then kicking out of them.

"Don't you want to go to the bedroom?" she asked him as he pressed her back against the door, his male hardness already finding her warm spot and moving against her.

"Later," he said huskily, then quickly, as their lips clung together, he lifted her until she was on her toes, then entered her, their bodies coalescing. She clung to him as the force of his lovemaking stunned her, lifting her quickly up into the heights of ecstasy where the heat inside of her was almost unbearable. She gave herself over to final surrender as a heady feeling washed over her and she felt a rapturous glow as she was engulfed by wave after wave of endless delight.

At last his body was motionless, only his head moving as his mouth placed butterfly kisses on her temples, her eyelids, her throat. He took her hand and led her into the living room to sit beside him on the couch, his arms enfolding her tenderly.

He put his hand under her chin and lifted her face to his. "Tell me, my love, were you thinking of Boots just then?"

"Of course," said Jess, snuggling closer to his warm naked body.

He pushed her away with a glare. "You *were* thinking of him?"

She moved away from him on the couch. "Were you testing me?"

"Maybe."

"I can't believe you're jealous of some character I made up."

The corners of his mouth twitched. "When you put it like that, it does sound asinine."

"It certainly does!"

"What *were* you thinking of?"

"Are you kidding? That was so fast, I didn't have

time to think." She moved so that her head was in his lap.

"I know; I couldn't wait. Next time will be slower."

"Tory, if you need to be reassured, you *are* the best lover I've ever had."

"I don't want to hear about them."

"You're not going to hear about them!"

"Anyway all the women tell me that," he said with a pleased smirk.

Jess got up from the couch, grabbed a pillow, slammed it over his head, then headed for the bathroom to take a shower.

Tory was close behind her. "Aha! The ice maiden can be jealous too!"

"I am *not* jealous," she said, turning on the water then stepping inside. She went to close the glass door, but he was right behind her, his arms moving around her waist.

"And I am *not* an ice maiden."

His hands were now soaping her body, causing delicious sensations. "No, I have to agree with that. In fact, you're feeling very warm to me."

He washed every inch of her lovingly, then dried her with a large brown towel before handing her his terry-cloth robe to wear.

"Now do you know what I'd like?" he asked, his eyes dancing.

"I have a pretty good idea," she answered.

"Can't you ever get your mind off sex, Jess?" he asked in a reproving manner.

"*Me?*"

"Yes, you. I was thinking what I'd like would be a nice, big piece of that chocolate cream pie we had the other night. I still have some left."

Jess tilted back her head and laughed in delight. "You are my kind of man, Tory Tyler the Third."

"That's what I've been trying to tell you, Jess."

Saturday it rained, and Jess was afraid that Tory, being so civilized, would not want to venture out in it. But after fixing her breakfast, he gave her gray sweat pants and a sweat shirt to put on, then, beneath a large black umbrella, took her down Third Avenue to Wings, where he bought her a pair of running shoes.

"I feel so comfortable," Jess kept telling him. "I'd like an outfit like this to wear when I'm writing. Or to sleep in when it gets cold."

"You can keep them," Tory told her.

"Really? I can take them home with me?"

"Since I know you're too cheap to buy yourself a sweat suit, yes."

He took her to his health club with him where he instructed her in the use of the equipment, then worked out himself while she amused herself lifting weights. Afterward they each ran two miles around the indoor track, and she had to admit he was in as good condition as she was. Which she thought was quite an achievement, considering the way he lived.

He wanted to take her out that night, but except for dinner at a Japanese restaurant on Second Avenue, they spent the evening in, playing backgammon for a while and then retiring early to bed to watch

Casablanca in comfort. She thought the movie ridiculously overromantic, but Tory swore it was a classic and not to be missed.

They made love once before the movie, twice afterward, and when Jess woke as usual at dawn, he rolled over in bed and they made love again. Surprisingly Jess was able to fall back to sleep, and the next time she awakened, it was almost noon and Tory was in the kitchen making coffee. While Jess watched, he made home-fried potatoes, mounds of scrambled eggs, and thickly buttered toast. After eating, she helped him clean up. He then opened his front door, brought in the Sunday *Times,* and they both settled happily on the floor, dividing the paper between them.

Jess made a few comments about so much advertising in a newspaper being immoral, Tory countered with a few choice remarks of his own, and then they both read silently until Jess's eyes hit upon an ad announcing her appearance in a Fifth Avenue bookstore the following Thursday.

"Look at this," she said to Tory, putting the paper in front of his nose.

"Umm, nice ad. Yes, that's the first thing scheduled; Phil will be signing autographed copies of his books there. Or rather *your* books."

Jess was dazzled by seeing her name in the paper. "Can I cut this out and keep it?" she asked him.

"Not until I've read that section."

She was still perusing the ad ten minutes later. "You know, I'm surprised people in New York would read westerns. I figured my readers all lived in the West."

"Most of them do, but there are a few here."

"Enough to make something like this worth-while?"

"There are a whole lot of people who will go to a bookstore to see *any* author in person," he assured her.

"Good. I'd hate for Phil to show up and be the only one."

"There'll be radio spots announcing it. I imagine we'll get a good turnout. Will he be ready by Thursday?"

"I don't know; that's not much time. Maybe I ought to work nights with him until then," she said, hoping Tory would try to dissuade her and insist they spend their nights together.

"That's a good idea," he agreed, much to her chagrin.

Feeling rather rebuffed, Jess said, "I guess my work is over Thursday then. I could fly home on Friday."

He put down his paper and reached for her hand. "You really going to leave me, Jess?"

Jess felt the unfamiliar sensation of tears forming behind her eyes. Don't you dare, she warned herself; you haven't cried since the fourth grade, don't start now. Then she thought of Mark's leaving her, and Robert's leaving her, and she pulled herself together.

"I'm not leaving you, Tory, I'm going home."

"I don't see the difference."

"My life's there."

He dropped her hand and sat up, arms folded around his knees. "Hell, Jess—we can't not be together; we were meant to be together!"

She felt the same way. "You could always come with me, Tory. Who says the woman always has to follow the man?"

He ran his fingers through his hair. "Tell me something, Jess. Your character, Boots Ryan. Would he just give up everything and follow a woman somewhere?"

Jess gave him a rueful look. "I write those books with a male readership in mind, Tory. And no, Boots wouldn't; he's too independent."

"How big's your cabin?"

Jess looked around. "Roughly about half the size of this room."

"Would you really want me to come live there with you?"

Jess's eyes took on a look of hope. "I'd love it."

"Just what do you envision me doing all day in that cabin while you write your books?"

Jess, who had never actually got far enough in her fantasies about Tory to envision that, didn't know what to say.

"And how would I support myself? Would you like me just living there off you like the family pet?"

Grasping at straws, Jess said, "Did you ever want to write a book, Tory?"

"No, I'm not one of those frustrated writers who turn to publishing instead. I love my work, Jess; I don't want to be anything else."

She shrugged despondently. "Then I guess it's a

stalemate." But even as she said it, an idea began to form in her head. "How about a compromise?" she asked him.

"What kind of a compromise?"

"How about meeting me halfway?"

"Tell me about it."

"Well, what's half the distance between here and Rocky Springs? Chicago? Saint Louis?"

He shook his head. "I don't know; I'd have to look at a map."

"Well, whatever it is, we could meet there weekends."

"That's a lot of commuting, Jess."

"Listen, from what Manny says, he spends at least fifteen hours a week commuting. It doesn't take nearly that amount of time to fly to Chicago and back. That way I could write all week, you could get all your work done during the week, and we could live together on weekends."

"It would be expensive, all that flying."

"You can afford it, Tory."

"I wasn't thinking about me. I was thinking about a certain miser I know."

Jess thought of her substantial savings account and knew she would spend it all if it meant seeing Tory every weekend. "I can afford it too, Tory. And I can always write more books."

"No, it's crazy; it won't work," he said decisively.

"Why not? I think it's a perfect plan!"

"It's not real, Jess. It's not even a commitment. Playing house in a strange city on weekends— No,

157

either you make up your mind that you want to be with me all the time, or—"

"Or what?" she asked in a small voice.

"Or I guess we might as well forget the whole thing."

Another ultimatum from another man, thought Jess. *And why did I ever think he'd be any different?* And to be honest, Jess thought, she wouldn't react any differently if she were in Tory's place. Why should he give up a business he built from scratch, a successful business, to go off and live in the wilds with some crazy writer? Just because she enjoyed being a hermit didn't mean everyone would.

Which meant that she'd only see him one more time alone before she left. She got up listlessly and went to the kitchen to pour herself another cup of coffee.

She was sitting at the kitchen table, staring into the cup, when Tory came up behind her and put his arms around her neck. "What's the matter, honey?"

"I'll only see you one more time then after tonight," she said softly.

His hands began lightly to massage the muscles in her neck, making her aware of her tenseness. "We still have tonight."

"That's not enough," said Jess, feeling tearful without the tears.

"It's important that Philip be ready."

"Listen, Tory, he's got almost total recall and is very good at improvising. . . ."

"We'll be together Thursday night, Jess. We'll

158

have a celebration, and on Friday I'll take you to the airport."

"Don't you want to see me before then?"

"Will you miss me?"

"Of course, I will."

"Good. Then maybe you'll find out in advance what it will be like when we're separated by half the country."

Jess shook off his hands and turned around, her eyes furious. "What is this, Tory, some kind of a test? You'll deprive me of your presence for three days and just maybe I'll decide not to leave New York after all?"

"It's worth a chance," he admitted.

"Well, it's not going to work, Tory. That's—that's emotional blackmail!"

"Come on, Jess. Let's not fight our last day together."

She got up out of the chair fast, almost tipping it over. "Maybe it would work even better if I left right now!"

He put out his arms and pulled her trembling body to his, patting her back as one would pat a child. "No, Jess, don't leave me now. Don't spoil the little time we have left to us."

And then he was kissing her, and Jess knew she wasn't going anywhere at all.

CHAPTER TEN

In the three days of intensive preparation they shared, Jess and Phil became good friends. He brought new things to her coaching she never would have thought of. What they both enjoyed most was what Phil called improvisations. They would act out different situations that could occur in a bookstore or during an interview, with Phil playing Jess and Jess playing either a fan or an interviewer.

Alli had also become a friend. She dropped by occasionally to see how they were doing and even joined in the improvisations. She was a natural comedian, breaking up Phil in the middle of his cowboy act and sending Jess sprawling on the floor with laughter.

It had started raining Sunday night and rained all week, which didn't do much to lift Jess's spirits. She was fine when Phil or Alli were around, but when she was alone, she didn't do much except think about Tory. He called once in a while to see how things were going, but never mentioned seeing her, only reminding her of their private celebration planned for Thursday night. Jess was too stubborn to beg, and the conversations usually terminated with her feeling unhappy and frustrated.

Because of the rain Jess and Phil were mostly confined to the hotel suite. They made ample use of room service, ordering food at odd hours of the day and night whenever the urge hit them. They talked at length of their respective childhoods and Jess even went so far as to invite Phil to her cabin if he ever felt the need to get away from it all. He told her he might take her up on it if he ever had the money, and he also promised to send her copies of any plays he wrote. She realized that Tory wasn't the only one she was going to miss when she left New York; she had enjoyed the companionship of Phil and Alli.

Hating to see Phil go out in the rain to return home every night, Jess had offered him a bed, but he had declined, pointing out to her that Tory would hardly approve. Wednesday night, though, when Alli decided she might as well sleep over, Phil said he would too, and they decided to have an old-fashioned slumber party.

Phil had never been to a slumber party, so Allison and Jess had to explain to him what they were all about.

"First of all," said Alli, "there has to be plenty of food. Usually it was hot dogs and French fries, which I doubt is on the Plaza's menu, but there's a Nedick's not far from here and I'll go out and pick some up. And pizza. We definitely have to have pizza."

"With anchovies," said Phil.

"Without anchovies," chorused the women.

"We always popped popcorn," said Jess.

161

"I think we'll have to do without popcorn, but I'll pick up plenty of candy bars," Allison promised.

"Hershey's with almonds," requested Phil.

"Licorice whips," said Jess.

"If I can find them," Alli told her.

"And liquor. We always sneaked drinks from our parents' liquor," Jess reminded her.

"That's no problem. We'll order up a bottle, then hide it in the closet to sneak from," giggled Alli.

"We should have champagne to celebrate," suggested Phil.

Alli gave him a stern look. "No champagne. It will give you a hangover, and we want you in perfect shape on Thursday."

"What about cigarettes?" asked Phil.

"We don't have to go that far," said Jess, knowing none of them smoked.

"What do we do besides eat and drink?" Phil asked, clearly amused by all the slumber party rules.

"All *we* ever did was talk about boys," admitted Alli.

"And tell dirty jokes," added Jess.

"Sounds good to me," said Phil, making them all laugh.

The slumber party was a resounding success. Jess thought that the hot dogs from Nedick's were the best she had ever eaten, chalking up another point for New York food. Alli went off her perpetual diet long enough to consume six candy bars in a row, and Phil, impressed by the expensive brand of whiskey the hotel had sent up, got roaringly drunk and not only told good jokes, but told them in several dialects.

They also talked about boys, if you could call Tory a boy. Phil's advice to her was to stay in New York and move in with Tory. "I'd move in with *anyone* to get an apartment like that in the city," he said, and Alli told him he had a point.

"Except Jess's problem isn't trying to find an apartment," she pointed out to him. "Personally I think it's terribly romantic that Jess is going back to her isolated cabin and renouncing love. *I'd* never be able to do it."

It didn't sound all that romantic to Jess; it just sounded lonely.

It was four in the morning before they finally went to sleep, Alli and Phil each in a bed and Jess in her bedroll on the floor.

Phil had to be at the bookstore at noon, and they got up with barely enough time to order breakfast and prepare him for his debut. When he came out of the bathroom wearing his jeans, a red wool shirt and his Stetson, Alli told him he was the spitting image of Jess Haggerty, that mangy old recluse of the West. She was all for drawing him a mustache with her eyebrow pencil, but Phil adamantly refused to let her near him.

They each gave him a kiss at the door and wished him success, then as soon as he left, Jess turned to Alli. "Do you want to go and spy on him?"

"I'd love to," breathed Alli. "Shall we disguise ourselves?"

163

"I don't have anything to disguise myself with," moaned Jess. "He's seen me in all my clothes."

Alli nodded. "We'll just have to hide behind stacks of books and not be seen."

"Would it make him nervous if he saw us?" asked Jess.

"Not if he's a good actor—and he is," Alli said, assuring her. She turned on the radio she had brought along to the slumber party and held her finger to her lips when the advertisement came on about Jess Haggerty appearing at the bookstore.

Jess got excited hearing her name on the radio, her eyes widening with delight.

"Are you sorry it's not going to be you there?" Alli asked her.

Jess looked at her in horror. "If I was hearing that and knew it was going to be *me,* I'd be so nervous, I wouldn't be able to eat!"

"For you that's really nervous," agreed Alli.

They left the hotel and headed for the bookstore, looking in all the shop windows on the way. Lunch-hour crowds were beginning to fill the streets, and up ahead they could see people going in and out of the bookstore.

They sneaked in the door, looking as furtive as shoplifters, and when they spotted Phil, they angled for a closer spot to watch him where they couldn't be seen.

He was chatting comfortably with people while he autographed their books, and Jess felt proud he was the one to play her in the store. He didn't look like a cowboy, just an intelligent man who happened to be from the West. Thank heavens Tory had gone along with her choice. She would be cringing now if they had used that garrulous old character actor.

They left the store without being seen by Phil, and Jess offered to buy Alli a farewell lunch.

"I won't say no to that," said Alli, heading down the street to an inexpensive but good restaurant.

Alli ordered her usual chef's salad, and Jess had a steak sandwich. Everything was over now, and she had a feeling of letdown. She'd probably never see Phil again; she was going to have to say good-bye to Alli in a few minutes; and after tonight it would be all over with Tory. She found herself thinking she might even miss New York. At least the food.

Alli watched as Jess ate cheesecake for dessert, then reached across the table and took her hand. "Sure you won't stay, Jess?"

Jess shook her head. "I've got to go home."

"I've never seen Tory so happy before," Alli mused. "I wonder how he'll take it when you leave."

"He'll survive," said Jess, hoping that she would.

"Oh, sure—we all survive, and there are other men in the world, and other women. But you two seemed so right for each other."

"Let's not talk about it," mumbled Jess, suddenly sorry she had eaten so much, because now her stomach was beginning to feel queasy.

Outside the restaurant Jess responded to Alli's kiss and hug, then turned and headed back to the hotel. She had several hours to kill before seeing Tory, and her nervousness seemed to be increasing by the moment. Things had seemed so simple to her in Wyoming, but here she felt torn apart. She couldn't wait to see Tory again, but part of her wanted to head straight home and avoid their final confrontation.

It was still raining, and the gray skies mirrored the way she felt. The rain on her face could almost be tears.

She knew what would happen—she knew exactly what would happen. She'd have dinner with him in his apartment. They would argue about any number of silly things, anything at all would do. And then he would take her in his arms and kiss her, and she would feel her insides melting from the pleasure she always felt when he touched her. And then they would make love, probably continue making it all night, and all the while he'd be begging her to stay and she would be practically torn in two by her refusal.

In the morning he would take her to the airport, and she just knew she'd never be able to get on that plane without dissolving into tears. And what good would that do? Did she want Tory's last memory of her to be her tear-stained face as she boarded the plane? Would she even *board* the plane? And if she didn't, if she stayed, how long would it be before she began regretting it? And why did she keep having to meet men who wanted everything *their* way?

She entered the hotel and went straight to her room. Without even thinking about it, she started to pack her backpack, stuffing her clothes inside without even folding them. The maid had been in and cleaned up the residue from the slumber party, and now the place looked impersonal.

166

She put her pack on her back and went down to the desk to check out. She didn't know whether she was doing the right thing or not. It might be the best way or it might be the coward's way, but she'd worry about that later.

She walked out of the hotel and hailed a taxi.

CHAPTER ELEVEN

Jess got off the plane tired, hungry, and cold. It had snowed while she was gone, and she hoped there'd be a pair of gloves in her Jeep. There wasn't; what's more, the Jeep had a dead battery. It was more than an hour before she got a garage to send a man out to recharge it for her, and by that time she was irritable as well as cold.

She debated staying in the city for the night and making the drive up the mountains in the morning, but now that she was in Wyoming, she was eager to get home. And she didn't think she could stand one more night in a hotel room. Alone.

The driving wasn't bad after the roads had been cleared, and the short distance from the road to her cabin was manageable with the Jeep. Drifts of snow had piled up against the door though, and it took her a good twenty minutes to clear it away before she could get inside.

The first thing she did was to find some fur-lined gloves to put on her cold hands; the second was to get the wood stove going to raise the temperature above freezing. She made a cup of coffee and huddled in her chair, using the cup more to warm her hands than anything else.

Every time she caught herself thinking about what she'd be doing in New York if she had stayed, she forced herself to think of other things. Except there wasn't much else to think about. She felt like an abandoned orphan—*worse* than an abandoned orphan.

"Quit feeling sorry for yourself," she finally said, liking the sound of her own voice. "You made your bed, now sleep in it!" Then she had to smile, because she didn't even have a bed.

When the cabin finally heated up to bearable, she got out of her clothes, into Tory's sweat suit, and wrapped herself in the bedroll on the floor. For no good reason except that she felt like it, she left the kerosene lamp burning all night. Waste of money or not, it made her feel better.

Morning was better. She looked out the window to see the snow-covered mountains and couldn't wait to get out in them. She dressed in ski pants, parka, and snow boots; put on coffee for later; then went outside. The sun was shining, the air tasted pure, and she found the tramp up the mountain trail had given her a wonderful sense of exhaustion by the time she reached the top. She caught a quick glimpse of a fox, and when she returned to the cabin, two deer were nearby, turning to melt into the trees when she approached.

She noticed she was low on both coffee and eggs when she fixed breakfast and decided to make a run into town before getting down to work on her new book. Over her second cup of coffee she caught herself thinking about New York. It didn't seem real to her now that she was back; more like some old movie she had seen and could now barely remember. She knew Tory would seem real, though, if she let herself think about him—which she wasn't about to do. "Right?" she said out loud. "Right," she answered.

Once in town she found she thought differently about Rocky Springs than she previously had. Before, it had always been a chore to have to drive in for supplies, but that morning she found herself being voluble with the people she met, friendlier than was her usual way. She went by the library and picked up a batch of mysteries to read, then even made a stop at the community college to pick up one of their catalogs. It might not be a bad idea to take a class, to make some friends. *Maybe my hermit days are numbered*, she caught herself thinking, then instantly dismissed the notion. It would probably just take a little time to get back to normal, that was all.

She decided not to work that day after all, but instead, spent the time cleaning the cabin and washing out some of her clothes. That night she read herself to sleep with one of the mysteries.

The next day she started her new book. The idea she had had before didn't seem to interest her now, and she thought about writing a book about Boots Ryan's being forced to take a trip to New York and all the difficulties he would encounter there. Then she decided that wasn't such a good idea after all because it probably wouldn't qualify as a western. She went back to her original idea and started to

170

write, but it didn't work out very well. Every time she wrote about Boots, she thought about Tory, and it was just too frustrating.

The next day she gave it up for good. Boots and Tory were now inextricably bound together in her mind; writing about one just brought to mind the other. It was just too painful at the moment, so she put the notes away and decided she'd give herself a couple of weeks before trying again.

But without writing, there was nothing much to do but just read the library books, one after another. All well written, all entertaining, but none of them earning her a living. She went hunting for rabbits and shot two; tried a little ice fishing but didn't catch anything; and made another trip to the library for some more books.

After a few days—after which she thought she was going to go crazy from inertia—she got an idea for a book. Not a western, but a mystery. About a lady detective who lived in a cabin in the Rockies and had to travel all the way to New York to solve a case. Too autobiographical, she told herself at first. Forget it, she thought—you don't even know New York that well. But she knew it better than she knew the Old West, having only read of that. And if she needed more background material, she could always go there and check it out.

Such thinking really didn't fool her one bit. Go there to check it out? Sure, and the first thing she'd do upon arriving would be to hightail it to Tory's office and throw herself in his arms. And that she didn't even want to think about! Because if she started thinking about being in his arms again, she was lost.

The idea of the mystery kept nagging at her and finally she sat down and began to plot it out on paper. It was a lot more difficult than writing a western, which made it a lot more of a challenge. And Jess liked challenges.

The outline was completed to her satisfaction and Chapter One started when she came back from her morning hike about a week after she had returned and found the familiar yellow envelope sticking out from under her door.

She cautiously picked it up, knowing full well whom it was from, then took it inside with her. She was still staring at the unopened envelope, hesitant to open it, as she drank her second cup of coffee. Then, deciding she *could* be wrong, and it *might* be from her parents, she ripped it open.

When she finally read it, she felt somewhat relieved. At least it wasn't about love or missing her or begging her to come back. All it said was for her to call him collect because they had to talk, and it was only signed with his name, not even *Love*.

The collect part annoyed her a little, as though she'd begrudge the money to call him. But not yet, she cautioned herself. Maybe in a few days she'd call just to see how the promotion with Phil went, but not yet. She was finally starting to get over him, and hearing his voice so soon would probably have disastrous effects. It helped not to be writing about Boots; it also helped to be engrossed in a new book, a different kind of book. Later, when she felt stronger, she would call.

A week later the second telegram arrived. This one read:

CALL ME COLLECT IMMEDIATELY.

Immediately? Not even a *please?* Typical male—thinking that she was just going to rush out and obey his orders. She was glad she didn't have a phone. The telegram didn't bother her much, but hearing his voice would probably be a whole other ballgame.

The next telegram two days later *was* a whole other ballgame. He was actually flying to Wyoming on Saturday and asked if she'd meet him at the airport. If not, it said, he'd find the way.

She knew there was no chance that Tory would find his way to her cabin without her help. He'd probably end up stranded in the snow and freeze to death, and she certainly didn't want that on her conscience. But why did he have to come here now? Just when she thought she was getting over him, he had to mess things up by showing up and when he left she'd have to start all over again. It just wasn't fair!

She drove into town to Western Union and sent off a telegram to him telling him not to come.

The next day his reply arrived:

I AM COMING.

Jess could have sworn she felt her heart leap when she saw Tory getting off the plane and heading in her direction. He was dressed in jeans, heavy boots that went almost to his knees, and a navy-blue ski jacket that set off his dark hair and eyes to perfection. She

173

didn't think she had ever seen such a beautiful sight and felt a tremendous longing to rush to him and fling herself into his arms, but caution prevailed, and she merely held out her hand when he got to her.

Tory was having none of that. He pulled her to him in a big hug, then stood back to look her over. "You look great, Jess. I guess I was hoping to find you thin and pining away."

"Now, why would I be pining away, Tory?" she asked him, not bothering to explain that she ate equally as much whether she was happy or unhappy or somewhere in between.

"Maybe because I was hoping you missed me as much as I missed you."

"Do you have any luggage?" she asked him, hoping to get off the subject of missing people.

"Nope. Decided to travel light like you. I also figured I could borrow my old sweat suit if I needed something else."

If he thought he was going to get his sweat suit back, he could think again. She practically lived in it.

"Do you have gloves?" she asked him, seeing his bare hands.

He pulled some out of his pockets to show her.

"Then you have all you need," she said, turning to lead him over to where her Jeep was parked.

"What are you doing here, Tory?" she asked as she pulled onto the highway.

"Well, the mountain wouldn't come to Mohammed . . ."

"I thought that was the other way around."

"It is, but it doesn't fit the other way around," he said, blowing on his hands to warm them up.

The traffic was light, and she figured she could make good time by hedging a little with the speed limit. "You'll never guess what I've been doing, Tory," she said to him, swerving around a truck and ignoring the fact he was clinging to the car door.

"Writing me love letters that you never sent?"

"No. Writing a mystery."

He gave her a look of astonishment. "Don't tell me you're not going to write westerns anymore."

"I'm just doing one, Tory—for fun. I found that writing about Boots—"

"Yes?"

"Forget it."

"You found that writing about Boots reminded you too much of me? Is that what you were going to say?"

"Nothing of the kind!"

"I don't believe you for a minute." He leaned over and put his arm around her.

"And keep your hands off me on these icy roads," she warned him.

"I don't think it's the ice you're worried about, Jess. What excuse are you going to use when we get to your cabin?"

"I wish you hadn't come," she said softly.

"I had to."

"*Had* to?"

"I couldn't concentrate on my work. Alli and Linda are threatening to quit because I've turned

175

into such a grouch. Manny's treating me like I've been sick. I even went to the ballet and hated it!"

Jess was touched by his admissions. Most of the men she had known would be acting real macho in a situation like this. They would never have let her see them vulnerable. "I've had a little trouble myself," she admitted.

"*You?* The indomitable snowwoman?"

"Not only can't I write a western, but I've been sneaking into town to eat at the Chinese restaurant, even though I have enough dried fish and venison to last me all winter."

The rest of the trip he told her how the promotion had gone. Phil had done well, and sales on her books had picked up in the New York area. "Phil gave me hell for not using you; said you'd be a natural."

Jess found herself laughing for the first time in ages. "I might have been a natural in the hotel room, but I would have been a royal flop in public. I never could have handled myself the way he did."

"Why did you run out on me that last night, Jess? Were you scared you'd change your mind and stay?"

"Something like that. I knew you'd really lay it on thick."

He chuckled. "I had fantasies of tying you up in my apartment and never letting you leave."

She flashed him a look. "Maybe I'll tie *you* up in my cabin."

He reached over and put his hand on her thigh, and it was all she could do not to pull the Jeep off the road and throw herself into his arms. There was no integrity in being alone when all she wanted was him.

"Maybe I wouldn't mind," he said softly.

They passed through a town in about the length of time it took Jess to say "This is Rocky Springs," and then they were out of it and heading up into the mountains.

Tory looked back through the rear window. "*That's* your metropolis?"

She nodded.

He whistled under his breath. "And you think Rocky Springs is too big?"

"Yes."

"No wonder you didn't like New York."

He commented on how beautiful the mountains were, and Jess knew he meant it. How could anyone not see their awesome beauty? It was getting dark by the time they got to the cabin, and Jess told him they'd wait until the next day to go for a hike, which he didn't seem sorry to postpone.

"How long are you staying?" she asked him, opening the door to the cabin and motioning him inside.

"I'm not sure yet. Until I've made up my mind, I guess."

Or until *she* did, she thought.

She was seeing the cabin through his eyes and making the natural comparison with his apartment, but all he said was "It looks comfortable."

She lighted the kerosene lamp, threw some more wood on the stove, then got out her one bottle of whiskey and offered him a drink. "I'm afraid I can't make you a Manhattan," she apologized.

"Whiskey's fine," he said, taking the proffered mug. He was looking around, not critically but with an interested air. "You really don't have a bed, do you?"

She shook her head. "I thought of buying something for you to sleep on, but decided it was a waste of money for just a couple of nights."

"I don't mind the floor. Not if it's with you."

Jess gulped down her whiskey and told herself not to be so nervous. This was Tory, the man she loved; of course, she was going to bed with him. Every chance she got, probably.

She turned to pour herself some more whiskey, and he came up behind her, putting his arms around her and his hands on her breasts. He kissed the top of her head, and she felt herself melting against him, excited at feeling the contours of his familiar body. She unbuttoned her shirt and moved his hands inside on her bare flesh. She gasped at the strength in his hands as he squeezed her soft flesh, then turned in his arms, reaching to pull his face down to hers and cover it with kisses. "Oh, Tory," she moaned. "Don't leave me. Don't ever leave me."

"I'm not going anywhere, Jess," he assured her, his hands caressing her body as his mouth sought hers with a hunger of its own. They kissed with passion as he gently lowered her body to the bare floor. He slowly undressed her, his eyes memorizing her body as it became naked, then quickly took off his own clothes as she watched through half-veiled eyes.

"This is love, not lust," he said to her as he knelt

178

astride her waiting body. "This is the closest two people in love can become, and I've never wanted it as much as I want it with you. Tell me you love me, Jess."

"I love you, Tory," she gasped with impatience, reaching up to pull him to her.

"Again."

"I love you; I'll always love you," she whispered in his ear as his body moved to meet hers and began to consume her. She arched to meet him, her body on fire in the cold cabin, her heart close to bursting with the love she felt for him.

He took her fiercely, exultantly, and she felt possessed. The floor was hard beneath her but her soft body urged him on to greater and greater heights, unmindful of the bruises it was sustaining. And here, alone, with no one within miles to hear them, she finally gave full vent to her passion, crying out as her senses exploded, leaving her feeling dissolved in their wake.

She slowly became aware of the weight of his body on hers, of the stillness within her, of her labored breathing.

"Are you all right, darling?" he whispered.

"Oh, Tory—that was incredible," she said when she could speak.

"I wasn't too rough for you?"

"No, I wanted you to be. I felt—for a while there I felt almost as if I were both of us at the same time, like we were really one. I've never felt like that before."

He moved so that he was beside her on the floor,

179

his arm cradling her head. "I guess something can be said for roughing it," he observed with a chuckle.

She kissed his chest, then reached for her shirt. Roughing it might be nice, but it was still very cold in the cabin. She sat up as she put it on. "I'm glad you're here," she said to him.

"I was counting on that, I guess."

"Are you hungry?"

"Well, you know those tiny meals they serve on planes. . . ."

She got up and put some more wood on the stove, thinking she should go out and bring in more, but not wanting to leave him for a moment. "What would you like?"

"What've you got?"

"Well, I have some fresh rabbit. I could make us a stew."

"Rabbit? Did you kill it?"

"This morning."

"Is it still in its skin?"

"No, I skinned it as soon as I killed it."

"God!" he exclaimed, covering his eyes with his arm.

"What's the matter, Tory?"

"I used to have rabbits as pets when I was a kid. How could you kill one of them?"

"They're not an endangered species, and they make good stew."

He got up from the floor and began to put his clothes on. "Couldn't you have told me it was chicken?"

180

"Why? Didn't you have pet chickens when you were a kid?"

He was about to reply when he suddenly stopped and laughed. "It's good to be fighting with you again, Jess. Incidentally where's the bathroom?"

She hoped he hadn't expected a real bathroom. "It's out in back. Take the flashlight by the door."

"What about a shower?"

"No shower, only a tub. If you want a bath you can haul it in after your trip to the outhouse."

He looked amused. "Just like in western movies." He put on his boots and went out the door as she stood watching him.

Civilized as he was, he at least didn't complain about the lack of amenities, she thought. In fact, he seemed to take roughing it very well. Probably much better than she would in his place. She hurried to cut up the rabbit before he came back; she didn't want Tory to get upset at the sight of a cute bunny being butchered. She set a pot simmering on the stove, put in the chunks of rabbit, then cut up potatoes and carrots and onions to go with it. She added a few spices, put on the cover, and was spreading her bed-roll on the floor for them to sit on when he came back in, dragging the tub behind him.

They talked until the stew was ready, and then picnicked on the floor. Tory took his first bite hesitantly, looking as though he might choke on it. But he nodded to show his approval. "It's good, Jess; you really know how to cook."

"Well, I don't know fancy things like Szechuan—"

"You're never going to let me forget that, are you?"

"Never!"

After dinner, while Jess heated water for the tub, Tory read the first chapter of her new book. "I think you have a good thing here," he finally said. "When you've finished it, I'll show it to an editor I know who handles mysteries. I think you should publish it under another name; *this* you might want to publicize yourself someday."

"It's not even finished yet, Tory. Maybe it will turn out awful."

"I don't think so."

"What name should I use?"

He gave her a slow smile. "What about Jessica Tyler?"

She looked up with a start and splashed water all over the floor. "Is that a proposal?"

"I just thought they sounded good together."

When the tub was filled, they both got in, their legs entwined in order to fit.

"This might even be better than a shower," said Tory, pulling her around so that she sat in his lap.

"Tory! Not in the tub!"

He moved beneath her. "Is there some law in Wyoming against sex in the tub?"

"Not that I know of."

"Then quit complaining."

Jess awakened at dawn filled with happiness. She felt like she could climb to the top of the mountains, wrestle single-handedly with a bear. She put the pot

182

on for coffee, then made a quick trip to the outhouse. When she got back, Tory was already up and looking out the window. He was stretching, and she wondered if his muscles were sore from sleeping on the floor.

"I saw some deer out there," he said, wonder in his voice.

"Sometimes they'll come right up to me and take food out of my hand," she told him.

"And then what? You shoot them?"

She poured a cup of coffee and handed it to him, hoping this wasn't the start of another argument. "I only shoot one a year, and only in season. And quit coming off like a vegetarian—steer will eat out of your hand, too, you know."

"Yeah, but they're not as pretty."

Jess tried to think of some animal Tory ate that was pretty, but couldn't come up with any. She was considering duck when he asked if she was going to show him the mountains that morning.

"If you want to see them."

He lifted a brow. "Did you think I came all the way out here just to see you?"

"I didn't know you were enamored of the Rockies."

"That's where you're wrong. It wasn't just circumstance that made me open a western publishing house, you know. I've always been fascinated by the West. I loved westerns when I was a kid, and I've read most of the writers."

They bundled up warm, and she led him up her favorite trail. He didn't complain that they were going almost straight uphill, but when they came to the waterfall that fed into the stream she used most often for fishing, she took pity on him and brushed the snow off a rock so that they could sit down and rest for a while. The view was breathtaking—all they could see in any direction was snow-covered mountains and dark green pines.

Tory made a snowball, then aimed it at a rock and threw it. "I can see why you love it," he said.

"Can you really?"

"I'd have to be blind not to see. You live in paradise, do you know that?"

She nodded happily.

His face look excited as it took in the view. "It looks just like Switzerland, and I always thought that was the prettiest natural scenery in the world."

She turned to him, her own eyes mirroring his excitement. "You've been to Switzerland?"

He nodded. "I went skiing there a couple of winters ago. It was incredible. Everything in Switzerland is clean and beautiful, and they have great restaurants."

She tried to remember Switzerland from pictures she had seen. "Where else have you been?"

"Most of Europe, Greece—Egypt once for two weeks. And Finland. Jess, you'd really love Finland. Snow as far as you can see."

"What about Paris? Have you been there?" She had always wanted to go to Paris ever since taking French in school. In fact, she had always wanted to travel, which seemed incongruous, considering she had once never even wanted to leave her cabin.

"You can't go to Europe and not see Paris," he was telling her. "It's incredibly beautiful—and the food!"

"Don't talk about food," she warned him. "We're at least an hour away from breakfast." She leaned against him, and he reached down and kissed her forehead.

He stood up and brushed the snow off his pants. "Shall we continue?"

She shook her head. "I'll take you in a different direction this afternoon. But now, since you've mentioned food, I'm starved."

He took one last look before they headed down. "I wish you could see it in the spring, Tory, when everything starts to bloom. Or the summer. It's so beautiful in the summer, and it never gets too hot."

"Or the fall when the leaves begin to turn?" he teased her. "I believe you, Jess. It's perfect."

After a breakfast of venison steak and eggs, Tory leaned back against the wall and regarded her seriously. "Okay, Jess—you win."

She smiled at his serious tone. "What do I win?"

"I'll move in with you. Give me two weeks to tie up loose business ends and sublet my apartment, then I'll arrive at your doorstep. If you'll still have me, that is."

She reached for his hands. "Are you serious?" In her wildest dreams she had never expected this of him.

"Perfectly serious. Why should you have paradise all to yourself?"

She clung to his hands, dazedly shaking her head.

185

"Of course, there will have to be a few changes. Nothing fancy; I wouldn't want to ruin your rugged decor."

She knew she'd agree to anything to keep him here. "What do you want to change?"

He pulled her over next to him, his arms going around her. "To start off with, how about a mattress on the floor? Not a whole bed, you understand; I don't want to corrupt you. Just a mattress. It would hurt my conscience to know I was bruising you every night."

"An air mattress would be good," she said, getting into the spirit of the game. A game she seemed to have won.

"And a comfortable chair. It doesn't have to be new or fancy, just something to read in. Maybe two, then we both could read in comfort."

She nodded, her eyes shining. "That would be nice, but do you think there's enough room?"

"That brings me to the next item. Unless you have deep objections, what would you think of adding on another room?" He got up and walked over to one of the walls, pointing to it. "We could break through here and extend it to the east, be able to watch the sun rise. We wouldn't have to call it a bedroom, but we could keep the mattress and our clothes in there. And if one of us wanted to sleep and the other didn't, we'd have some privacy."

Jess was on her feet now, too excited to stay still. "I don't mind at all. That's a great idea. What else would you like?"

He put his hands on her shoulders and looked

down at her. "That's enough; we don't want to get too spoiled. Oh, no. One more thing. Another straight chair so that we can both work at the same time."

She came back down to earth. "What kind of work will you do?"

"I've been giving that a lot of thought. I'll still own half the business, so I'll have enough money to live on. More than enough. I'll let Alli take over most of my work, but I don't see why I couldn't do some editing from here. Or even read manuscripts. And if it doesn't work out, I'll just sell out my half of the business to Manny and think of something else to do."

"Oh, Tory, you'd really do this for me?"

"Without you the rest is meaningless."

She hugged him, tears beginning to stream down her face. She had heard of people being so happy they cried, but she had never experienced it before. "Then you don't have to do it," she told him.

"I don't have to do what?"

"It's enough that you *want* to do it, that you're *willing* to do it. I think that's all I really needed to hear."

He stroked her hair, his hand gentle. "What are you talking about, love?"

"I'll move to New York with you, Tory."

He lifted her head and grinned at her. "Is that a proposal?"

"Yes."

"I accept."

She smiled with delight. "I think I've outgrown being a hermit anyway."

"When did you find that out?"

"When I missed the food in New York."

His hand brushed the hair back from her shining face. "What else did you miss?"

"Alli. And Phil."

"What else?"

She thought for a moment. "Central Park. Oh, and hot and cold running water."

"That's all?"

"And you, of course," she said, reaching up to bring his face down for a kiss.

He pulled her down to the floor with him and held her close. "Listen, Jess, we can still build onto the cabin—we can even modernize it and come here for our vacations."

"You know I'd love that, but not *every* vacation."

"I thought you'd miss it here."

"I'd rather see Paris," she told him as visions of her and Tory together in that romantic city filled her head.

"I'd love to show you Paris," he said.

"And Finland."

"We'll go there whenever you want. You know what? We could even go on an African safari."

She chuckled. "I can't see you shooting animals, Tory."

"I'll watch you. And Scotland. The fishing's supposed to be great there. And we could go on hiking trips through England."

"How about Hawaii?"

188

"I've never been to Hawaii."

"My parents live there," she told him.

"Then we'll go there on our honeymoon."

"Is that a proposal?"

He laughed. "No. As I recall, you proposed earlier."

She got to her feet and went over to her footlocker, opened it up, and began to pack her backpack.

"What are you doing?" he asked from the floor.

"I'm getting ready to go."

"We could stay here a few days."

She shook her head. "No, I want to start our new life now."

"Afraid you'll change your mind?"

"I'll never change my mind about how I feel about you, Tory."

She doused the fire in the wood stove as he got ready, then took his hand and went out the door, closing it behind her and never looking back.

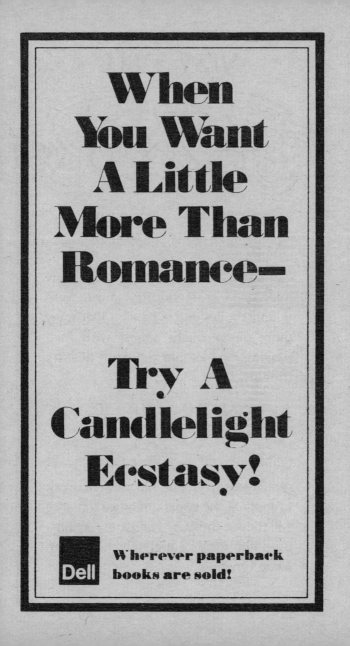

NEW DELL

LOVERS AND PRETENDERS,
by Prudence Martin
$2.50

Christine and Paul—looking for new lives on a cross-country jaunt, were bound by lies and a passion that grew more dangerously honest with each passing day. Would the truth destroy their love?

WARMED BY THE FIRE,
by Donna Kimel Vitek
$2.50

When malicious gossip forces Juliet to switch jobs from one television network to another, she swears an office romance will never threaten her career again—until she meets superstar anchorman Marc Tyner.